The Mystery of the Seine

(annotated)

By G. H. Teed

Cover by Arthur Jones

Edited by Doug Frizzle

First published in The Sexton Blake Library,
1st series, No. 366; 31 Jan 1925

Stillwoods Edition

Stillwoods.Blogspot.Ca

Catalogue Information:
Title: The Mystery of the Seine (annotated)
Author: G. H. Teed (1886-1938)
Illustrated by: Arthur Jones
Edited by: Doug Frizzle (1949-...)
First published in The Sexton Blake Library, 1st series, No. 366, 31 Jan 1925.
This Edition by: Stillwoods, 2024
ISBN Canada: 978-1-998819-42-3
Blog: Stillwoods.Blogspot.Ca
Author Blog: http://ghteed.blogspot.com/
Old Storefront: http://www.lulu.com/spotlight/lulubook22

https://tinyurl.com/ve25d42s This link should go to a spreadsheet of all known Teed stories. The list is annotated with various information on the stories and my progress with recapturing the work. The library of Teed's stories increases almost weekly. Check at Lulu.Com for the earlier publications. Search for Teed. /drf

Keywords: Sexton Blake, Poissy, France, The Three Musketeers.

Cautionary Note: This series of books by Stillwoods are intended to make the stories of G. H. Teed, born in New Brunswick, Canada, available to collectors and researchers. The editor, or rather digitizer has not altered the original publication.

This story may contain language and racial terms that are not appropriate today. I apologize for them; I know that the author was using his voice to excite and entertain an adventurous English audience. These works were published from 82 to 110 years ago. Most every work has characters of redeeming ethnicity within.

I hope you enjoy and share these stories; I have.

Doug Frizzle

Contains unacceptable racial terminology

A long tale of Detective Adventures in France featuring The Three Musketeers and others.

Blake is invited by the French Sûreté to investigate a series of fantastic robberies.

Other content: The Crook Specialist (article)

Introduction to the Annotated Edition

- Facsimile Reproduction
- Supplementary Information
- Historical Context
- Collectors' Commentary
- Author Biographical Notes
- Teed's indebtedness, so moves to Paris

This Stillwoods collection is about the author G. H. Teed. The great majority of his 500+ stories were written anonymously. They also, at the time, were issued under copyright —under the Sexton Blake banner. Teed wrote from 1913 until his death at the end of 1938. Since most of these works were anonymous, no-one knew he was a Canadian —or at least I have never seen a mention.

Teed's novels appeared in 'pulps' mostly —magazines with cheap paper, and issued mostly on a weekly basis. In original format, they are difficult to obtain today in undamaged condition. And they can be expensive!

Included in the ancillary material is the usual advertising for the next weekly issue and an article 'The Crook Specialist'.

Digitized by Doug Frizzle. This story may also have also been digitized by others. Often those copies revise offensive terminology; I have retained the original terms only to indicate acceptable language of the day. Again I apologize to anyone that might be offended.

Teed's indebtedness forces him to live in Paris./drf
Much of what follows came from a fellow publisher/researcher whose work is far superior to my own efforts, but he is not directly

researching Teed's life so I am reporting this. Any errors are mine, any credit goes to Nico Lorenzutti.

From Surrey Mirror 22 June 1917:

WOLDINGHAM.

A JOURNALIST'S AFFAIRS.—The affairs of George Hamilton Teed, journalist, of Deanest, Woldingham, were before the Registrar at Croydon Bankruptcy Court, on Thursday. His liabilities are given as £2,099. Assets nil. He described himself as a native of New Brunswick. After leaving home he went to Central America, where he caught malarial fever, and later returned home. In 1912 he came to England, and since then had devoted himself to journalistic work, writing for magazines issued by the Amalgamated Press. He started borrowing from money lenders in 1915. He borrowed £60 on his wedding day. Before that he had borrowed from stewards at his club, paying back for a loan of £5 for a week £6. He might have told his wife's brother something about his means. He did say, and it was true, that he belonged to a wealthy Canadian family. They possessed some land on the West Coast, and before the war the Government intended erecting a harbour there. He also told his brother-in-law that at the outbreak of the war he drove a motor car in Paris which the French Government commandeered. At his wife's suggestion he borrowed some money from his brother-in-law to pay back £5 a week. He knew he had not been careful and threw his money about. He also borrowed £298 from a friend of his wife's family. He hoped to put by money weekly to repay it. He reckoned he earned between £1,200 and £1,500 yearly. A skunk coat he bought for a lady in 1914 he paid £27 for; one for his wife that in 1915 cost £31 was not paid for. He bought his wife an engagement ring for £40. It was pawned for £15. His wife also pawned some of her things and gave him £15 to pay an account with. He did not pay it. He put the expenses of self and wife at £1,400 a year, and reckoned that last year he earned £1,250 from the Amalgamated Press.—The Official Receiver thought he had much overrated his income. One cause of his trouble was the illness of his wife. He had to take her to Cornwall. He now lived in a furnished house costing £3 10s. a week.—Examination adjourned.

WOLDINGHAM.

A JOURNALIST'S AFFAIRS. —The affairs of George Hamilton Teed, journalist, of Deanest, Woldingham, were before the Registrar at Croydon Bankruptcy Court, on Thursday. His liabilities are given as £2,099. Assets nil. He described himself as a native of New Brunswick. After leaving home he went to Central America, where he caught malarial fever, and later returned home. In 1912 he came to England, and since then had devoted himself to journalistic work, writing for magazines issued by the Amalgamated Press. He started borrowing from money lenders in 1915. He borrowed £60 on his wedding day. Before that he had borrowed from stewards at his club, paying back for a loan of £5 for a week £6. He might have told his wife's brother something about his means. He did say, and it was true, that he belonged to a

wealthy Canadian family. They possessed some land on the West Coast, and before the War the Government intended erecting a harbour there. He also told his brother-in-law that at the outbreak of the war he drove a motor car in Paris which the French Government commandeered. At his wife's suggestion he borrowed some money from his brother-in-law to pay back £5 a week. He knew he had not been careful and threw his money about. He also borrowed £98 from a friend of his wife's family. He hoped to put by money weekly to repay it. He reckoned he earned between £1,200 and £1,500 yearly. A skunk coat he bought for a lady in 1914 he paid £27 for; one for his wife that in 1915 cost £31 was not paid for. He bought his wife an engagement ring for £40. It was pawned for £15. His wife also pawned some of her things and gave him £15 to pay an account with. He did not pay it. He put the expenses of self and wife at £1,400 a year, and reckoned that last year he earned £1,250 from the Amalgamated Press.—The Official Receiver thought he had much overrated his income. One cause of his trouble was the illness of his wife. He had to take her to Cornwall. He now lived in a furnished house costing £3 10s. a week.—Examination adjourned.

And from Sutton Epsom Advertiser, 19 October 1917:

CROYDON BANKRUPTCY COURT.

Thursday, Oct. 18th.—Before the Registrar, Major J. E. Fox.

A THIRD OF HIS INCOME

In the case of George Hever Hamilton Teed, of Deanest, Woldingham, story writer, of the Amalgamated Press, whose public examination we detailed in previous issues, the Official Receiver stated that the debtor was earning over a thousand a year, and he asked for an order to be made against the Amalgamated Press to pay to the Official Receiver 33⅓ of debtor's earnings.

Debtor had no objection to such an order being made. He only wanted to do the square thing.

The Registrar said that he would make the order.

Debtor said that he had not been doing any work for two months. He was under treatment and might have to undergo an operation.

Under the circumstances the Registrar directed the order to come into force on January 1st.

CROYDON BANKRUPTCY COURT. Thursday, Oct. 18th.— Before the Registrar, Major J. E. Fox.

A THIRD OF HIS INCOME

In the case of George Hever Hamilton Teed, of Deanest, Woldingham, story writer, of the Amalgamated Press, whose public examination we detailed in previous issues, the Official Receiver stated that the debtor was earning over a thousand a year, and he asked for an order to be made against, the Amalgamated Press to pay to the Official Receiver 33½ of debtor's earnings.

Debtor had no objection to such an order being made. Be only wanted to do the square thing.

The Registrar said that he would make the order.

Debtor said that he had not been doing any work for two months. He was under treatment and might have to undergo an operation.

Under the circumstances the Registrar directed the order to come into force on January 1st.

From Nick Lorenzutti:
Hey Doug,

I found these while doing some research. Teed had some financial problems in 1917. On January 1st, 1918 the court was going to do the equivalent of garnishing his wages from the Amalgamated Press.

On January 6th he enrolled in the Army. He was discharged 77 days later for heath reasons.
Seems like his army service was more to outrun creditors than serve his country :)

He was 2,099 £ in debt. That's about 183,000 in modern £.
Pretty amazing

In Canada...
2100£ in 1917 □ 183000£ in 2024 □ $320,000 CAD
1250£ □ 190,000 annual salary in CAD...

It also might explain his later travels and living abroad.../drf

Story contains unacceptable racial terminology

Some stories we are working to bring back to life:

The Mystery of the Seine
The Quest of the Grey Panther
The Secret of the Five Rings
The Mystery of the Girl in Blue
The Crook's Decoy
The Adventure of the Two Devils
The House of the Wooden Lanterns
The Affair of the Empress's Little Finger
The Case of the Stricken Outpost
Doomed to the Dragon
The Adventure of the Yellow Beetle
The Hand of Vengeance
The Case of the German Colony
The Latin Quarter Mysteries
Rogues of the Revontazin
The Crime of Stanley Trail
The Affair of the Walnut Desk
The Mystery Man from Manila
The Secret
The Case of the Missing Athlete
The Emerald Necklace
The Treasure of Bloody Gut
The Crime of the Creek
The Banker's Box
Honolulu Lure
The Silent Woman
Perilous Pearls
The Case of the Scented Orchid
Poisoned Blossoms
The House of Fear
The Clue of the Two Straws
The Mystery of the Tramp Steamer
The Crest of the Flood

I have gotten way behind because of some rules by others!/drf

viii

CHAPTER 1.   The Movements of Monsieur Jules Fernaud —
Deliberate Murder.

IT five o'clock in the evening of a beautiful September day, Monsieur Jules Fernaud, a prominent member of the Paris Bourse, and a gentleman who did considerable business as a private banker, left his office in the Rue St. Marc, near the bourse, and walked at a leisurely pace in the direction of the Sentier station of the Metro or Underground.

In one hand he carried a small black leather bag which one might have observed was fitted with a lock of more strength than is usually the case with bags of that size. Under the other arm —the left —he clutched a leather portfolio, and in his left hand was a copy of the third edition of the "Intransigeant," containing the closing prices of the day on the bourse.

The banker did not stop for an aperitif at the corner cafe, where it was usually his custom to spend a few minutes on his way home, but with a nod to the garcon, who saluted him with considerable deference, he continued his way, and descended the steps of the Sentier station.

He purchased a first-class ticket there, and descended another flight of stairs to the platform, at which the east-bound train would stop. He had but a few moments to wait before a train came along, and, still clutching his belongings tightly, the banker joined the rush for the carriage.

He did not proceed, however, any great distance on the east-bound train for he got out at the next station and made his way, by means of the connecting passage to another level, where a west-bound train would take him across the river to the left bank. He succeeded in getting a seat in this train, and with his bag placed between his feet took occasion to glance at the news.

The train rattled along past the markets station, then under the river, by way of the Ile de la Cite and the Place St. Michel, and so up towards the Latin Quarter.

It was at the station called Vavin that Monsieur Fernaud got out, and, on emerging at the top of the stairs, found himself exactly at the point where the Boulevard Raspail crosses the famous Boulevard Montparnasse, and directly in front of the well-known Latin Quarter cafe, the Rotonde, which faces the even better known Cafe du Dome across on the other corner of Montparnasse.

But again the banker passed the rows of tables on the terrace without stopping, and continued on foot down the Boulevard Raspail until he came to a big and obviously newly erected block of flats, a little way down. He entered here, and with a word to the concierge as he passed the lodge, opened the door of the electric lift, stepped inside, closed the door after him, and pressed the controlling button marked "2."

He got out at the second floor, just opposite the entrance to one of the flats, and stood for a moment to send the lift down again. Then he fumbled for his keys, selected one, and thrust it in the lock. The next moment he opened the door and stepped inside.

He was now in a wide, long hall, well furnished with good rugs, good furniture, and good pictures, at one end of which was a really fine old stained-glass window, through which the westering sun was gleaming with a subdued and mellowed light.

As he closed the door after him, he set the bag on the floor, laid the portfolio on a chair, and, reaching out, pressed a button.

A few seconds later a door at the other end of the hall opened, and an elderly manservant appeared. At sight of his master, he hurried forward to take his hat and gloves. He would have taken the bag and the portfolio, too, but his master indicated, by a gesture, that he would carry those himself.

The servant opened a door near at hand, and disappeared, while the banker picked up the two leather receptacles and proceeded towards a door on the left about halfway down the hall. He opened this, and stepped into a most luxuriously-furnished library-study, and yet which, like the hall, had a touch of cold formality about the tout ensemble that told its own tale.

It was the utter lack of anything that would have indicated the presence of a woman in the place, and, indeed, the whole flat revealed the same austere atmosphere, for Monsieur Fernaud was a bachelor, and, with the exception of an elderly maiden sister, who visited him twice a year, no woman, other than the concierge and her daughter, ever entered the flat.

Not that the banker was too old even now to consider marriage. He was perhaps forty-four or forty-five years of age, of a somewhat heavy, florid type, but exceedingly well-preserved, and quick and vigorous in his movements.

Like a great many Parisians of the professional and business classes, he wore a luxuriant beard, which in his case was of a chestnut brown, slightly touched with grey, and carefully trimmed and curled in deference to its owner's pride in it. He was getting a little thin on the crown, but that was not very noticeable, and altogether Monsieur Fernaud was an attractive-looking gentleman.

In his business he was genial, but shrewd, and, although he did not operate on as great a scale as many, he was a consistent manipulator, and his credit was listed at a high figure.

On entering his library, he laid the portfolio on the wide, flat mahogany desk, and set the bag on the floor. Then he sat down, and, lighting a cigarette, waited until there was a tap at the door and the manservant entered.

"Monsieur is going to-night, then?" asked the man.

"Yes, Gaston. I shall leave from the Gare de Lyon at half-past eight. You have my luggage packed?"

"Yes, monsieur, with the exception of a few articles about which I wish to ask monsieur. It can be completed in a few moments."

"Good! And for dinner —you have prepared something?"

"Yes, monsieur. It will be ready in half an hour."

"That is well, for I wish to dine early. Bring me an aperitif, Gaston, and then call me when dinner is ready. I have some writing to do before I go."

"Very good, monsieur."

With that the man retreated, but came back a few minutes later, bearing a silver tray, on which reposed a bottle of vermouth, another of cassis, a syphon of soda, and a small pail of freshly broken ice.

From a carved cabinet in one corner he selected a thin Venetian goblet, such as his master favoured when he drank an aperitif at home, and nearly half filled it with vermouth. Then he poured in a small quantity of the cassis, added a lump of ice, and filled up the rest of the glass from the syphon. He served this on the end of the desk, and, with a bow, withdrew.

Monsieur Jules Fernaud intended making a brief business visit to Dijon, where he had banking correspondents and several clients who operated on the bourse on a fairly heavy scale.

It was the banker's custom to pay a visit to that city every three months, the time spent usually occupying three or four days. During that time he would transact certain matters with his agents, and take the opportunity of meeting as many of his clients as possible. It was on such occasions that he would have a three-monthly settlement with his agents, and, if money were due from him to them, he would take it along with him in the small, but strongly-made, leather bag which he had brought home with him that evening.

On the other hand, the leather bag would go along just the same, for, in the event of his receiving money on balance, instead of paying, he would accommodate the notes and bills in the same bag.

And that was the journey he intended making on this evening in September, when he had left his office a little earlier than usual.

This was one of the occasions, too, when he would pay instead of receive, and, against the liquidation of those balances, there was in the bag at the time a sum in bank-notes, negotiable bills, and bearer bonds of something over two million francs, or, roughly, about thirty thousand pounds in English money.

Quite a tidy amount, and quite large enough for the banker to take the risk of packing it along with him, and thus save the ordinary bank transfer charges, which on that sum would amount to an appreciable item.

He wrote several short letters to business friends in Paris, advising them of his contemplated journey, and occasionally took a sip of the drink at his elbow.

He had just finished sealing one of the missives when the man came to announce that dinner was served, so, after a brief visit to the bath-room to wash his hands, he went into the dining-room for his solitary repast.

It was just a little after seven when he finished, and, after a brief consultation with his servant about certain articles to be packed, he returned to the library, smoked a cigar, and wrote one or two more letters. At exactly eight o'clock he rang for the man, and instructed him to go out and find a taxi.

The servant departed at once, and, while he was waiting, Monsieur Fernaud slipped into a light travelling-coat, also putting on a round soft hat, such as is favoured by many French business men.

Then he walked along towards the front door, to wait. It was just as he did so that there came a tapping on the heavy ground-glass panel, and, thinking it was Gaston —although his brows rose a little at the thought that the man had been very quick about finding the cab — he turned the brass knob of the spring lock and opened the door.

But it was not Gaston who stood outside. It was, instead, a young man in what the banker knew where garments cut only by a very exclusive and very expensive tailor. Over a suit of some brownish material was a long, loose motoring dust-coat of fawn, and on his head the young man wore a leather cap, the visor of which was pulled well down over the eyes. As the banker stood in a questioning attitude, the young man said:

"Monsieur Fernaud?"

"I am he, monsieur," answered the banker. "But, if you have come to see me on business, I am afraid I can give you no time this evening, for I am on the point of leaving the city."

"I am aware of that," said the other coolly. "That is why I have come, monsieur. And there will be plenty of time for the business I have to transact with you."

As he spoke these words one hand came from the side-pocket of his dust-coat, and the amazed banker found himself looking into the muzzle of an automatic pistol, over the barrel of which had been fitted a contraption which he guessed vaguely was a silencer. He had heard of the things somewhere or other.

"But —but, monsieur, what does this mean?" he cried.

"Back into the hall!" snapped the young man and, as he advanced, the banker perforce gave way. Once inside, the eyes beneath the visor of the leather cap darted this way and that, and he gave a slight exclamation as his gaze fell on the leather bag which had been placed beside a larger travelling bag.

"I have come for that bag," he said curtly. "If you are ready to hand it over without a fuss I shall not harm you. If not —"

And he paused significantly.

The banker's mind worked quickly. He was no coward, and yet he knew himself to be utterly helpless in the face of that threatening pistol, while something in the young man's attitude told him he meant business. On the ether hand, there was the manservant who had gone to fetch a taxi. He should be returning almost at any moment now.

If he could make himself heard Gaston might realise that something was wrong, and get hold of the husband of the concierge. It was with this thought in his mind and because he was not going to hand over the bag containing the money without putting up some sort of struggle that he opened his mouth to give a yell.

But the sound never came. Even as the vocal cords were

tightening for the effort, even as the voice was on the very point of coming into function, the young man gave a snarl and pulled the trigger of the automatic, just once.

The banker gave one short cough as a small hole appeared in the very centre of his forehead, and then he crashed to the floor with a pellet of lead lodged in the inner depths of his brain. The young man had done the killing as cold-bloodedly as he would have swept a mosquito from the back of his hand.

He stepped coolly over the crumpled form of the dead banker and caught up the bag. Then he turned and opened the door which he had closed behind him on entering.

He took little pains to suppress the sound of his movements, but instead of pressing the button to bring up the lift he went down by the stairs. As he did so the wire cables of the lift began to shake, and a second later the lift shot up with a single occupant in it. It was Gaston returning from finding the taxi.

The young man reached the ground floor just as the lift reached the second. Then he turned to the right and passed out coolly, merely glancing at the concierge's lodge as he went by. At the kerb, in front of where the taxi had drawn up, was a long, powerful-looking roadster. At the wheel sat another young man, dressed much after the fashion of the first. He glanced up casually as the other crossed the pavement and his eyes rested on the bag. He waited until the bag had been tossed into the tonneau and the other climbed in beside him.

Then he pressed his foot on the self-starter, and with the cut-out wide open he sent the car out into the Boulevard Raspail, turning almost on two wheels. He swung to the right there, and away they went roaring down the boulevard in the direction of the Seine just as a dazed and incredulous manservant was gazing with horror upon the dead body of his master.

CHAPTER 2. *After the Big Society Function —Another Hold-up —Conflicting Evidence.*

JUST a week after the hold-up, killing and robbery at the flat of M. Jules Fernaud in the Boulevard Raspail a second daring act of banditry occurred in Paris. On this occasion it was staged in the Champs Elysees, and again cost a human life.

In some respects it was even more ruthless and cold-blooded than the other, and the booty which the authors got away with was nothing less than the famous Borosov necklace, which is known to every jewel dealer and connoisseur in Europe. The details as known to the Paris police followed this sequence.

Prince and Princess Borosov, a semi-royal Russian couple, who had been living in the French capital since the downfall of the old order in Russia, had spent the latter part of the summer at Deauville, the fashionable resort on the Normandy coast.

Before leaving for that place, however, certain of the princess' jewels had been placed in the bank for safekeeping, and among them was the famous necklace, so-called the Borosov piece, which had graced some of the most brilliant functions of the old Imperial Russian court.

They had returned to Paris early in September, but it was not until well on in the month that the princess took some of her jewels out of the bank, among these being the necklace in question.

Her reason for doing so was an approaching affair at the Opera, which was to be given in honour of a visiting royal personage, which would be attended by the cream of the Parisian haute monde.

The withdrawal from the bank took place just two days before the ball, and until that evening the jewels remained in a small, private safe in a dressing-room between the princess' apartment and those of her husband.

Owing to an important meeting among the supporters of the Grand Duke Nicholas, who had just then issued a manifesto to his fellow exiles, the prince could not accompany the princess to the opera, but an elderly companion, who was a distant relative, went along with her.

As is usual on such occasions, the whole of the Place de l'Opera was crowded that evening, and when the function was over, there was a good deal of confusion among the cars in trying to get in from the parking spots to the great staircase, which was packed with those waiting for their vehicles.

Under these circumstances it was some time after the princess and her companion had emerged that they managed to find their car, and there was another delay while the chauffeur threaded his way slowly out of the press, and finally managed to get into the Rue de la Paix, which was comparatively deserted.

From there he drove through the Place Vendome, and the Rue Castiglione to the Rue de Rivoli, where he turned to the right and made for the Place de la Concorde.

It was then getting close to midnight, and there was still plenty of traffic travelling in each direction, more particularly up and down the Champs Elysees, to and from the cabaret-restaurants in that thoroughfare, or from the theatres, making towards the all-night places in Montmartre.

The Borosov "hotel" was in the Avenue du Bois de Boulogne, and then in taking the route of the Champs Elysees the chauffeur was using the most direct way of reaching his destination.

The big car rolled along at a steady pace up the fast traffic section of the avenue, passing the Hermitage and Claridges on the right, the Champs Elysees and the Carlton on the left, and pulling on towards the Etoile and the Arc de Triomphe.

It was just when the car was opposite the Astoria —which is now used by the Reparations Commission —that the driver suddenly uttered a sharp exclamation of annoyance, and jammed on his brakes.

He was just in time to avoid a collision with another car that had shot out from a side street on the right and had, in apparently the most reckless fashion, driven straight across their course.

It was a low, powerful-looking roadster containing three persons —one at the wheel, and two, whose open coats showed the gleam of white dress shirts, in the back.

The driver of this vehicle had also jammed on his brakes, with the result that the big roadster had come to a stop exactly across the bows of the Borosov limousine, so to say, and with less than twelve inches separating the radiator of the one from the side door of the other.

At the very moment of stopping the two men in the back of the roadster stood up, and then with one accord jumped out.

Other traffic coming behind had seen that something was wrong, and was pulling out to one side a little lower down, and was speeding past in the centre left of the avenue. In near the kerb there was no slow traffic at that hour of the night.

The two men walked quickly towards the limousine, and while one stood by the driver's seat, apologising in French for the delay, the other opened the door and lifted his opera hat to the two women inside.

"I am desolated that this has happened," he said courteously, addressing the princess. "It was entirely the fault of my driver, who, however, was but carrying out instructions. It gives me a thousand regrets, your highness, but I really must ask you to hand over the necklace which you are wearing. If you will look through the window you will see that we are not to be trifled with. You will notice that your man has already been dealt with."

And as the cool words dripped like ice, the horrified princess and her companion gazed ahead to see the chauffeur suddenly slump down in his seat and lurch over sideways. At the same moment a subdued report reached them, but they did not know that it was caused by an automatic pistol which had been fitted with a silencer.

But they did know that they were being held up in the most open and one of the most aristocratic thoroughfares in Paris. It seemed incredible that such a thing could happen with so much traffic passing up and down, with scores of persons within hail. And yet it had been done, and was being done, and there was something in the icy quality of the voice of the man who stood at the half-open door of the car that told the princess she could expect no mercy.

Exactly what had happened to the chauffeur she couldn't make out, but it was plain that no assistance could be expected from him. But she was no coward and did not intend to give up her jewels without an effort to frustrate the attempt of the bandits.

She opened her mouth to scream, and, at the same instant, raised her arm to try and lower the plate-glass panel beside her, but before she could accomplish either, the man at the door had leant inside and the next instant her scream was throttled in her throat, the while her arm was jerked down and twisted painfully against her side.

The elderly companion had slipped quietly into a faint, and, for the next few moments, the princess was only vaguely aware of what was going on. She realised, in a way, that her necklace was being torn from her, that she had been hurled back heavily into the corner of the car, and then that the man was gone. She struggled mightily to bring her outraged senses back into function, and a few moments later managed to get to her feet.

She stumbled out into the road, conscious that the car that had been drawn across in front of the limousine was no longer there. Then she gave vent to scream after scream, and, at the sight and sound, the occupants of several cars up-bound, drew in to see what was wrong.

Two gentlemen, one a member of the French senate, as he informed the police later, who had also been at the function at the Opera, were the first to reach the distracted lady. While one supported her she tried to tell them what had happened, but at first her words formed simply incoherent phrases, and it was not until someone produced a silver flask of brandy that she was able to make them understand.

In the meantime, a couple of constables, or "agents," had appeared, and while one of them took the particulars, the other made the shocking discovery that the chauffeur had been shot through the heart.

This caused a general movement of the curious towards the front of the car, but one of the agents must have realised the need for quick action if the bandits were to be caught, for, disregarding the dead man for the moment, he made sharp and pertinent inquiries as to what had become of the car driven by the bandits.

From one source and another he collected sufficient information to get a fairly accurate idea of the type of car to be sought for, and a taxi-driver who had just come across the Etoile from the Avenue de la Grande Armee stated that such a car had passed him there, going at a terrific pace in the direction of Neuilly!

On hearing this, the senator immediately offered his car to be used in the pursuit, and, half a dozen more agents, as well as a sub-inspector, having come up by then, the offer was accepted and the chase begun.

Another car was placed at the disposal of the princess and her companion, who were then driven home. Her car was taken charge of by the police, together with the body of the murdered chauffeur, and, after some names and addresses had been taken, the crowd broke up and went off about its own affairs.

That, roughly, is the report contained in the papers the day after the hold-up, and the evening journals were able to add that the fugitive car had been traced by the police pursuers over the bridge at Neuilly, and out along the main road there as far as the village of Le Sec, on the edge of the forest of St. Germain.

There, however, it had been lost, and, with the exception of one journal that drew a somewhat lengthy comparison between the hold-up on the Champs Elysees and that at the flat of the late M. Jules Fernaud, in the Boulevard Raspail, the public heard scarcely any more of the affair.

This did not mean, however, that the Sûreté was not working on the case —on both, in fact. On the contrary. From M. Dupuis, the Prefect down to the newest recruit to the Criminal Investigation Department, every brain was busy with the two problems, and not only those two, but others, for, although the public did not know, the officials at the Sûreté were convinced that both hold-ups had been the work of the same persons, and not only that, but that they formed but a part of a series of daring acts of banditry which had been occupying the attention of the Sûreté for some time.

As far as could be gathered from the material in the possession of the police, the outbreak had begun in the early part of July, and up to the date of the hold-up of the Princess Borosov in the Champs Elysees, towards the end of September, the list was a formidable one, with not a single arrest made so far.

It seemed to have begun with an attack upon a small manufacturing jeweller in the northern suburb of Levallois. On this occasion, the man was on the point of leaving his office one evening when two young men entered his office and held him up.

At the time he had beside him a bag containing a fairly large quantity of valuable gold and set pieces, far more valuable than he was accustomed to take away with him.

It seemed, then, that this must have come to the knowledge of those who held him up, and the police, at the time, put it down as the work of some local criminals who had got hold of the information. But following that, there was a mid-morning hold-up of the cashier of a large manufacturing firm at Boulogne-sur-Seine, and certain features caused the police to suspect some connection between it and the other.

The cashier had been to the bank to draw the week's wages for the factory hands, and was returning when he was held up. On this occasion automatics fitted with silencers were brought into play, and although the cashier was wounded in two places, he recovered and was able to give a general description of his assailants.

In some respects this tallied with that furnished by the first victim, although there were important variations which made the descriptions of little practical use to the police. For the first time they heard of a low-slung, powerful car as being used by the bandits, and a description of this was sent out to all agents and gendarmes.

Following that, a car returning from Deauville had been held up near the forest of St. Germain, and the occupants, three Paris business men, who had been playing heavily at the casino in Deauville, were relieved of money and jewels to the tune of something like eight hundred thousand francs.

There was no gun work on this occasion, but automatics had been produced, and it was the unanimous opinion of the victims that they would have been brought into play had any resistance been attempted.

For the first time, the police were able to get some sort of definite description of the bandits, and the car on which they could work.

With regard to the bandits (on this occasion there were two in the back of the car they had used and one at the wheel) they learned enough to make from the various details some sort of composite portrait of each, although, while the type of car was again stated to be a low-slung, powerful roadster, it was described, on this occasion, as dark blue in colour, whereas the cashier of the works in Boulogne-sur-Seine had stated most positively that it was a bright red.

They knew fairly well now, however, that the bandits were all young men, apparently of some degree of social pretension and education, if one could judge by their manners and voices, but whether of French or foreign birth it was impossible to say.

The three business men all agreed that there was something foreign in their appearance, but the French used by the two who had been most active in the holdup was as polished and as pure in accent as that of any French academician.

The next occurrence brought to the notice of the police was the daring hold-up of a branch of one of the big banks in a small town just beyond the racing centre of Maisons-Laffitte.

The branch in this town was one that was only opened for business on two days in the week. On these days it was the custom of the agent and a clerk to go down from Paris, taking with them sufficient funds to handle what business passed through, and of course on their return journey the same evening they carried, in addition, all the deposits made during the day.

On the occasion of the hold-up, business for the day was just over, and the agent and clerk were preparing to catch the train back to Paris, when two young men entered the bank and covered them with automatic pistols.

The agent at once jumped for his own weapon, but before he had taken a single full stride one of the bandits had fired, and he had dropped dead with a bullet in his heart.

Even in the stress of the moment the clerk noticed that the weapons were fitted with silencers, and that, of course, accounted for the fact that the sound was not heard by anyone outside the premises although at the time the cobbled street was fairly crowded with both wheeled and foot traffic.

On seeing the fate of his superior the clerk put up no resistance and allowed the robbers to seize the funds and decamp with them.

As they raced out he ran after them to give the alarm, and saw that they drove off in a low-slung, powerful roadster which he described most positively as dark blue in colour. He noticed then, too, another man at the wheel, but as he wore heavy motoring goggles and a leather cap drawn down over his eyes the clerk was vague in his description.

But from what he was able to tell the local police, and later, the man from the Sûreté, who was sent to interrogate him, was sufficient for the officials at the Sûreté to suspect strongly that the robbery was the work of the same bandits whom they were seeking.

Following the bank raid there was a lull, and although the police were working incessantly they could not seem to get hold of any definite thread to give them a lead. In their very boldness the bandits had, in a way, confounded those who sought them.

Then came the killing of the banker, Jules Fernaud, in his flat just off the Boulevard Raspail. The only witnesses available there were the concierge and his wife and the taxi man whom Gaston, the banker's servant, had fetched.

The concierge and his wife stated that they took little notice of the man who came in and asked for Monsieur Fernaud. He had stood out of the light, and neither had seen his features very plainly.

They had informed him that the banker's apartment was on the second floor, and also that his servant had just stepped out. He had

13

thanked them, and then entering the automatic lift had ascended.

That was all they could tell, except that the wife of the concierge had seen him pass out, and was quite sure he had descended the stairs on foot. The taxi man said he had noticed a low-slung powerful car at the kerb as he drove up. There was a man at the wheel, and shortly after a well-dressed young man had come out of the building, and after throwing a bag in the back had climbed in.

Then the car had gone off at a reckless rate, turning to the right in the Boulevard Raspail. But he was quite positive that the colour of the car was grey, and stuck to this statement.

Another brief lull and then the hold-up of Princess Borosov in the Champs Elysees. That, in its way, was the most spectacular of the lot, and as they examined the evidence available, the officials at the Sûreté came to the unanimous conclusion that again the same bandits were at work.

And on this occasion Prince Borosov and certain gentlemen high up in the government, insisted that something must be done at once to run the bandits to earth.

That was the puzzle which the worried Prefect had to wrestle with. It was easy enough to say: "Find me those bandits and put them behind the bars." But where could one put one's hands on them? Where could they have their lair? Once he could discover that item M. Dupuis would not be slow in acting.

CHAPTER 3. *Sexton Blake Called to French Capital —The Explanation of the Prefect of the Paris Sûreté.*

MR. SEXTON BLAKE, the eminent London criminologist, was sitting in conference with M. Dupuis, Prefect of the Paris Sûreté. His arrival in Paris was the outcome of a personal letter from the Prefect asking him, if possible, to cross the Channel, and, as M. Dupuis had put it, lend his distinguished aid in a problem that was occupying the French police at the moment.

Blake knew before he left England that the problem was one dealing with the sensational series of hold-ups that had been occurring in and about the French capital recently; and in London, too, there had been some evidence of the work being done by the Sûreté, for the assistance of Scotland Yard had also been sought.

It was believed possible that the criminals may have succeeded in getting across to England, but if this were the case, Scotland Yard had, so far, been unable to find any trace of them.

Mr. Dupuis himself believed that they were still in France, for on the very day before Sexton Blake had arrived one of his men, a young sub-inspector, who had come to Paris from the Lyons force, and was already making considerable impression on his superiors, had reported certain things which seemed to justify this opinion.

It made, so to say, a curtain to the chapter of crimes which the Prefect was describing to Blake and capped what theorising he was able to do.

He had begun with the first hold-up that had come to the notice of the police —the robbing of the small manufacturing jeweller in the suburb of Levallois. From that he had gone on to a relation of the subsequent robberies and killings, completing his recital by a detailed account of the spectacular hold-up of the Princess Borosov in the Champs Elysees.

To all this Sexton Blake listened with the closest attention, making an occasional mental note now and then, or fixing on some point about which he would ask a question later. When he had described the various crimes, and read off a catalogue of the loot the bandits had got away with, he took up the big police dossier dealing with the work done, to date, by the various detectives who had been assigned to the investigation. It was a bulky affair, that dossier, for, since the killing of Jules Fernaud, the banker in his flat off the

Boulevard Raspail, the Prefect had put additional men on the case, and after the Borosov affair had added still another half dozen. As he opened the dossier he glanced up at Blake and said:

"I shall not attempt to read all the reports here now, M. Blake. It would only tend to confuse you. But perhaps you will take the dossier along to your hotel with you and go through it there. I shall, however, give you a brief resume of what has been done so far."

Blake nodded.

"I shall take it back with me, with pleasure," he assured the Prefect. "But it would be as well, if you gave me, as you suggest, a resume of what has been done so far."

"It begins with the preliminary inquiries made at the time of the hold-up in Levallois," went on M. Dupuis. "At the time we were inclined to the view that the robbery was the work of local criminals, but after the affair in Boulogne-sur-Seine we changed that opinion. Of course, as you know, there are certain rowdy and —er —difficult elements in Levallois and some of the other manufacturing suburbs, and it is not the first time such a thing has occurred there. But, as I have said, we altered our minds when the other robbery took place in Boulogne-sur-Seine.

"With regard to those two occurrences we have, I regret to say, not been able to gather much evidence of a reliable nature. There are one or two obvious points which appear to connect the two, or rather, to make it appear that they were the work of the same persons. But the other crimes yield a little more evidence, and I may say that we have sifted every item with the greatest care. Those results you will find detailed here in the dossier.

"One thing which seems to be a common factor to every crime is that the same type of motor car was used by the bandits. You will notice, M. Blake, that I use the word 'type' and do not say the same car. I shall explain why. From the evidence we have examined it seems fairly safe to assume that the type of car was the same, if it wasn't the same, in every case, for all the reports agree on that point. It is described by the victims as well as other witnesses in almost the identical words in each case —as a low-slung, powerful roadster.

"But there the evidence shows differences, for while one witness affirms that it was black, another affirms positively that it was red, whereas still another is equally sure it was blue, and, again, another is emphatic that it was grey in colour. Even allowing for mistakes due to the excitement of the moment and the margin of error in the evidence offered by the ordinary person, it does seem to me that these statements are not as confusing as they would appear, but that a car of different colour was used on each occasion."

"Pardon, monsieur," put in Blake. "On that point I presume you have taken into account the possibility that the car was repainted after each hold-up —that is to say, that the same car was really used on each occasion."

"That has received my attention, M. Blake. And personally I am inclined to think that is exactly what was done. That the persons were the same each time seems beyond reasonable doubt, and that there were not more than three is also fairly certain. All three did not always take part in a hold-up. One only carried out the crime in the flat of the late Monsieur Fernaud, although a companion waited in the car for him. Again, there have been only two, and, as in the case of the hold-up in the forest of St. Germain and of the Princess Borosov, all three have been present. So much for that phase of it, monsieur.

"Now I shall pass over the general work that has been done. It is all here for you to read. But I wish to speak to you of the investigations that have been made by one member of my corps —a young man from Lyons —and presently I shall have him in here for you to meet him, for, if you consent to give us your aid, and I shall feel highly honoured if you will, then I propose placing this man under your orders. He is the only one who has struck something in any way definite, but even he is now at a dead end. I shall explain.

"You will find as you peruse the dossier, monsieur, that where any of the hold-ups occurred outside Paris, they were on all occasions in an area that is entirely to the north of the city. Levallois is a northern suburb; Boulogne-sur-Seine adjoins Neuilly. The forest of St. Germain is to the north. The small town where the bank raid took place is also to the north. Thus you will see all their operations have been confined, so far, to that area.

"Now another point. In relating the details of the Borosov affair to you, you will recall that when the car containing the bandits made off, it went up the Champs Elysees, and, according to reliable evidence, after crossing the Etoile, went down the Avenue de la Grande Armee. By patient work we have managed to trace a car answering to the description of the one used by the bandits, over the bridge at Neuilly and out the main road to the north as far as a small place on the edge of the forest of St. Germain known as Le Sec. At that point the trail is lost.

"But there is the significance of the holdup which took place in the forest, and the robbing of the bank in the other small town near the edge of the forest. I say significant because it shows that this area is well-known and principally attractive to the bandits. Your own deductive faculties will tell you why."

"I presume you mean because somewhere in that area the bandits have their lair." remarked Blake.

"Precisely, monsieur. And this young man of whom I have spoken has put in a report —he brought it in only yesterday —which confirms that view. He has been doing quiet work for some time through the area of which we have been speaking. Needless to say, a most thorough combing out of the forest of St. Germain has taken place, and a large force of special guards have been scattered throughout it. I am convinced that the bandits are not using any part of the forest as a hiding-place, although I thought at first such might be the case.

"As I was saying, this young man has been at work out there. He has been hanging about the various small towns and villages on the outskirts of the forest, and the night before last he struck what looked like a clue. He was, at the time, in the small town of Poissy, which, as you know, monsieur, is on the bank of the Seine, just five kilometres above the better-known town of Villennes and about forty kilometres from Paris."

"Oh, yes, indeed," said Blake, with a reminiscent smile. "I know Poissy quite well. I have angled there for the elusive goujon and the wily eel. It has quite a reputation as a fishing centre."

"That is so, monsieur —a very old and historical little town and one of the most beautiful spots on the Seine."

"It is that," agreed Blake fervently.

"Well, monsieur, it is in that town that my young inspector came upon what seemed to him to be a clue, and which, he is convinced, he proved later was undoubtedly one. He followed it up at the cost of no little physical discomfort, for in the course of his inquiries he received what you call in your country, a severe beating. Under ordinary circumstances, police reprisals would have been taken at once, but he is, you understand, working in secret, and nothing has been done. But later on —yes, later on —he shall have full satisfaction." And as he uttered the words the Prefect smiled grimly.

"To proceed, monsieur. As I have said, my man followed up this clue. Unfortunately, at the time he was on foot, and for a time it seemed as if the persons he had under suspicion would elude him. But he picked up the trail again and, after that, came upon some most interesting things, although before he could get hold of anything definite he was, as I have said, beaten up. And he was forced to come away from the place with nothing very tangible to show for his pains. But I have here the full written report of what occurred, and as he tells it better than I can repeat it, I am going to ask you to read it. While you are doing so, M. Blake, I shall leave you for a few minutes in order to attend to one or two matters outside. Here is the report."

As he finished speaking he took some sheets of paper from the dossier and handed them to Blake. Then he rose, and as the door closed after him Blake lit a fresh cigarette and settled back to read the strange and intriguing report handed in by the young sub-inspector of whom the Prefect had spoken.

THE first part of the report which Sexton Blake settled down to read dealt with the movements, over some days, of Sub-inspector Coignet, the young officer who had written it. These paragraphs detailed how he had visited several towns and villages on the outskirts of the forest of St. Germain, but contained nothing pertinent to the experience he had had at Poissy.

It was not until he came to the second page that Blake began to get to the meat of it, so to speak. And it was when the young man spoke of having left the town of Acheres, which lies between Poissy and Maisons-Laffitte, that he began to approach the events which had occurred at the former place.

"I left the town of Acheres about seven o'clock in the evening," the report ran (although he had written in the time as about "nineteen o'clock," after the French fashion of calling the hours). "It was just dusk," the writing continued, "and as the town of Poissy-sur-Seine, my next destination, was only a few kilometres distant, I decided to make my way there on foot in order to enter the place as unobserved as possible.

"I reached the edge of the town about eight o'clock the same evening, and took my way down into it by way of the Rue Meissenier which runs past the old Abbey demense and the ancient church. From the open space in front of the church I made my way by a very old, narrow lane into another old street that brought me out in front of the Maine (Town Hall) at exactly sixteen minutes after eight by the clock in the tower over the Mairie. The main street of the town passes here, and from the corner where I paused I could see a road called the Rue de Paris, which is part of the main Havre-Paris road, as it ran in both directions.

"I followed the road down a dip beneath where a railway bridge crossed, and then round a sharp, blind corner, at the immediate approach to the bridge which crosses the Seine just there to the strand or river front of the town. On the right is a hotel-restaurant, called L'Esturgeon, from the terrace of which the bank of the river is clear of any buildings for about a quarter of a mile to a point where private property runs to the sheer edge of the water.

"On the left is a small hotel known as the Rendezvous des

Pecheurs (Fishermen's Headquarters) and, just beyond, other small restaurants and cafes followed by private houses. The strand itself is planted with lines of small chestnut trees. I decided to put up at the small hotel Rendezvous des Pecheurs, and, under the name which I assumed, took a room.

"Before proceeding with my investigations in that town I took a meal in the hotel, and took careful note of the persons patronising the place, and also of what conversation I overheard. There was nothing worthy of note in either. After dinner I walked the length of the strand, noticing as I did so that moored to the bank were several floats where boats could be hired, and three very large houseboats which were used as municipal washhouses.

"I then retraced my steps, and passed the first hotel which I have mentioned. This I entered, and on the pretence of ordering a bottle of beer had a look round. It was plain to me that it was a place of good type and the proprietaire and his family were solid respectable French citizens.

"From that place I passed again round the blind corner at the entrance to the bridge, and returned past the Mairie. It was then twenty minutes past nine, but even at that early hour the streets were almost deserted and most of the shops and cafes were closed. The majority of the inhabitants are hard-working people, who retire at an early hour.

"I passed the Mairie, and as I came to the corner where the Rue de Paris makes a sharp turn I found a small Cafe still open. I noticed that the patronne was an elderly woman of clean and neat appearance, and, knowing that she would have all the local facts and gossip at her fingertips, I seated myself on the terrace and ordered white wine. I was, as far as I could see, the only client, and I had no difficulty in engaging the woman in conversation.

"I sounded her on local affairs, and found that, at the time, the chief topic of conversation was of a murder which took place in a small village across the river a few days ago, and which I presume has been reported at the Sûreté. I brought the talk round to the hold-up and robbery of the branch of the B— Bank in the town of J—, a few miles from Poissy, and the woman talked freely enough. But as far as I could gather, little was known in the place other than what had appeared in the papers, and certainly the local gossip is far more vague than the facts in the possession of the police.

"I was still engaged in conversation with this woman when from along a road which ran at a tangent from the street where I was sitting came the flare of the headlights of a powerful motor-car. I watched this vehicle approach, but not until it had swung out of a direct line could I see clearly, for the lights blinded my vision. It turned sharply to the left as it approached me, and as it did so, I noticed that it was a low-slung, powerful roadster, containing three figures, all men, I judged, one at the driving-wheel, and two in the back. The colour appeared to me to be either black, dark blue, or dark purple.

"It turned the corner at high speed, and went up the Rue de Paris in the direction of Paris. It soon disappeared from view in a bend of the street, but there was something about the vehicle and its occupants that recalled the description of the car and the bandits for which the Sûreté is searching. I waited to ask the woman if she recognised the car as a local one. She informed me that she thought she had seen it before on a few occasions, but could not be sure.

"Then I put down some money, and ran up the hill after it. I kept after it for some time by the sound of the exhaust, but soon that stopped suddenly, and I was forced to choose my way by chance. The street there runs uphill clear to the market-place, which is about half a mile from the Mairie, and beyond that continues on into the country. It is the same road by which I walked from Acheres.

"I had almost reached the market-place when I met a gendarme, the first person I had seen since leaving the cafe. I asked him if a car had passed him, but he informed me that none had done so, and, as I am under strict orders to keep my identity secret even from the police, I did not risk questioning him further.

"I turned and retraced my steps then, and came to the conclusion, as I went down the hill, that the car must have turned to the right, making towards either the old church or one of the residential streets in that neighbourhood. While I had entered the town by the main road above the market-place, I had taken a side-turning that had brought me past the old Abbey demesne and the church, so, in an effort to locate the car, I walked along these streets.

"I stopped from time to time to listen, and once I met a man, whom I questioned. He informed me that he had noticed a car passing through the church place, but could give me no description of it or the occupants, so I did not hold him in conversation. I covered every street in that part of the town, but without avail, and at last I retraced my steps to the little cafe at the corner of the Mairie. It was still open, so I again sat down in order to plan my next step.

"I had a feeling that the car I had seen was the very one which has been eluding us, and in that case one or more of the occupants must have been bandits. I make no excuse for having allowed it to elude me, except that it was not until it turned the corner that I could see it distinctly, and I was in possession of no bicycle or other vehicle by which I could follow more quickly.

"I remained at the little cafe until half-past ten, and was then on the point of leaving, when I saw three figures coming down the Rue de Paris on foot. As they approached nearer I saw that they wore long motoring coats, and two of them had on leather caps. The third wore a soft hat well pulled down. They struck me as being very similar in appearance to the men I had seen in the car which had passed a little while before, and I watched them as they turned the corner and kept on towards the bridge.

"The woman of the cafe was inside at that time, and I could not call her to ask her if she had seen them before, without attracting their attention. I left some money on the table, and as soon as they had disappeared in the dip under the railway-crossing I followed. As I reached the edge of the dip I could see them going up the other side, and when I reached that point they were just passing between the old buildings at the approach to the bridge, which means they had passed the blind corner to which I have previously referred, without turning down to the strand.

"I kept on after them, and kept them in sight until they had covered the first three or four spans of the bridge. Then all three suddenly disappeared. It will be necessary to give a brief explanation of how this happened. A glance at the map of that part of the Seine will show that, as in many other parts, the river is broken by numerous small islands, which lie all the way from above Poissy down to beyond Villennes. These islands are all heavily wooded, and are mostly private property.

"At Poissy, just opposite to the hotel L'Esturgeon, to which I have also referred, there are three of these small islands; two lying side by side, one being possibly five or six acres in extent, and the other only about a quarter of an acre, with a small water passage between them. The third lies just above this pair, and is separated from them by another channel, some forty feet in width, and with a strong backing up of the river current at that spot.

"It is this third island which abuts on to the bridge, and, indeed, is used for the support of one of the stone piers. It is private property, in so far as its occupation is concerned, and as I went along, wondering what had become of the three men I had been following, I discovered that in the trees on this small island there is a cafe of sorts. It is reached by a flight of steps leading down from the bridge, and it was evidently this way that the trio had disappeared.

"I could see that the place had a light burning, although there didn't seem to be much business going on. I resolved to descend, and did so.

"After passing through a small place under the trees where iron tables had been set out, I entered a bar, and at the first glance knew the place was an unsavoury resort. There were three men in one corner who looked like Italians, and, as the woman at the other cafe had told me, there was an Italian colony of factory labourers on the other side of the river, I concluded that these men came from there.

"There were a man and a woman in another corner, and behind the bar was the man I presumed to be the proprietaire. He was of an unusual type to find in this part of France, and for the benefit of my colleagues I shall describe him. He was, I should think, from North Africa, either Algeria, Morocco, or Tunis but not of pure Arab or Berber stock, for his features were distinctly negroid. He was a giant of a fellow, of most forbidding appearance and villainous countenance. At some time one cheek had been opened by a terrible knife-cut, and in healing this had drawn down the corner of one eye until it gave him a grotesque and sinister expression.

"He was dressed in only shirt and loose pants, and I knew that he was examining me closely as I walked to the bar. (I should like to suggest here that it might be suggested to the Poissy police that this place should be investigated when we have completed our inquiries in that part.)

"He seemed disinclined to serve me, but did not actually refuse, and, as I sipped my drink, I looked about for the three men who had disappeared from the bridge. I could see no signs of them, but, as I judged there to be a room at the back as well as others overhead, I knew it was quite possible they were in one of those apartments. It was a strange place, in my opinion, for men of their appearance to go to at that hour of the night, and my suspicions were becoming stronger each moment.

"I could not request to be served in a private room. This would have raised a question at once. I knew I should have to wait until my men came out again, or else give the chase up for the time, and try to pick up the trail again when they left the place. But an unlooked-for chance came my way and I took it.

"I had been in the place for about a quarter of an hour when there was a pounding on the floor above the bar. The big black hammered an answer on the wall, and then walked to a door leading to the back. As he opened it, I could see a small room with some tables in it, and another door, partially open, which seemed to lead into the grounds at the back, for I could see trees.

"There was, I discovered later, a staircase in one corner which was invisible to me then, and I could hear the black mounting it. Then a door slammed, and I took a chance of walking into the back room. It was empty, but as no one made any attempt to stop me, I kept on to the open door on the other side. I looked through the opening, and found that, as I had thought, it opened into the back of the place.

"I could see, near at hand, the water all round, and, as I stood there, from somewhere on my left a soft whistle sounded. I stepped out and listened. The whistle sounded again, and above my head a window was raised. A voice, which I knew to belong to the black, said something which I could not catch, and then the window closed.

"From where I stood at the edge of the little island, could not have been more than forty or fifty feet at most, but the trees were very thick, and there was a good deal of cover despite the restricted area. I knew that in that cover, some place, was the person who had whistled, and I made up my mind to find out. Up till then I thought the men I had been following were in an upstairs room, but now I wasn't so sure, and in any case, the whole atmosphere of the place was such as to demand investigation.

"I stepped forward, and began to work my way through the trees. I had gone half a dozen paces when a sound behind me caused me to run back. As I did so I saw one of the Italians I had seen in the bar enter the back room and approach the bottom of the stairs. I heard his voice as he called something up, and following that I saw the big black come down the stairs, covering the distance in a single leap.

"He dashed through the door towards where I was standing, and with a string of oaths made for me. I dodged, and ran towards the bank, intending, if necessary, to dive in and swim across to the other bank, or the small boat pontoon which I had noticed in front of the L'Esturgeon. But before I could reach the edge, there was a crashing of bushes in front of me, and I found myself attacked by two men.

"In some way, I know not how, I managed to slip under their arms, and gained another yard or so, but by now the black had arrived on the scene, and all three rushed me. I stood up to them as well as possible, but I was hopelessly outmatched, and once in the grip of the black I was helpless. I could feel his hands at my throat, and I knew that he intended to choke the life out of me.

"I could do nothing, and I had given myself up for lost when one of the others spoke to him, and his fingers loosened their hold. Then I heard him say that they would examine what I had in my pockets in order to find out who I was. If they did that I knew that it only meant prolonging the moment of my killing, and if I was to escape, my only hope was to get clear then.

"While the black held me, I allowed myself to go limp, then, as he shifted his hold a little, I slid down through his arms, delivered a savatte, and sprang for the river. I gained it, and plunged in. I found myself at once in the current, and was swept across the narrow channel to one of the small islands. I touched this, and, turning, saw that I was being pursued.

"I climbed up some crumbling revetment, and ran through the trees to the other side of the island. I plunged in again there, and as I swam towards one of the floats which was moored just below L'Esturgeon, I gave cries for help. This apparently caused them to turn back, for the pursuit was abandoned, and I landed safely.

"I made my way along the bank, and concealed myself near the approach to the bridge to watch for the three men to come away. I saw the others leave about midnight, and then followed the sound of a motor-boat. I guessed that my quarry had left in that way, and as the sound died away up the river, I knew it was useless to wait longer. I then returned to the small hotel where I was staying, and after making out my report retired to bed.

"This report I shall get away by early post to-morrow, and have only to add that during the coming evening I shall pursue my investigations at the house on the river, for I am more strongly suspicious than ever that I have struck a promising clue. If possible, I should be glad if another man could be detailed to this spot to assist me.

"Receive, Monsieur le Prefect,
"My most humble and distinguished salutations,
"(Signed) GASTON COIGNET."

But after the completion of the main report, the sub-inspector had evidently opened it the next morning to add a few words, for in a postscript Blake read:

"Monsieur le Prefect,
"I have the honour to acknowledge the receipt of your letter containing instructions to report in Paris on Thursday. I shall present myself at the Sûreté at nine o'clock in the morning of that day as instructed.
"Receive, monsieur, etc.,"

Blake laid the papers down, and lit another cigarette.
"The report is clear and comprehensive enough," he muttered. "This young man has brains, and shows some considerable intelligence. I am just as well pleased that Tinker and I shall have him working with us. He is modest enough about his own exploits, but I fancy it must have been a choice little rough and tumble he had on that island at the bridge. This is Thursday, so he should be waiting below now."

Blake glanced towards the door just then. It had opened, and the Prefect entered. He said nothing until he had seated himself, but then he turned to Blake and the latter saw that his face was very grave.

"You have read the report, monsieur?" he asked.

"Oui, monsieur. I have found it most interesting. I presume we shall hear in person from this officer what happened at the house on the river last night. I note that he says in this report that he intended paying the place another visit which would have been last night."

"We shall hear nothing more from that gallant young officer, Monsieur Blake," said the Prefect. "I am just in receipt of a telephone message from the commissaire of police at Poissy in which he informs me that the body of a young man was found in the river between Poissy and Villennes this morning. By certain code papers on the person of the man found, he has identified him as Sub-inspector Coignet, of the Sûreté. But that is not all. He was not drowned. They have already discovered that there is no water in the lungs, but what they have found is that his neck was broken, and the skull hammered to splinters. It is cold-blooded murder, M. Blake!"

"UNDER the circumstances, M. Blake, I feel it to be only fair that I should withdraw my invitation to you to lend us your assistance in this case. The murder of poor Coignet proves that these criminals are ready to kill on the slightest provocation. They could not have known that Coignet was of the police.

"At most they could have had but a vague suspicion that he had any more than ordinary curiosity regarding the house on the island of which he wrote in his report.

"We do not know that he paid a second visit to the place, nor was the commissaire at Poissy able to give me any details of the crime. All he was able to state was that the body had been found by some fishermen floating in the river about half way between Poissy and Villennes, and, by certain secret ciphers among the papers, he knew that the victim was a man from the Sûreté.

"But we can conclude that he did visit the house on the island last night as he intended, and was brutally murdered as a result. Therefore, you can see, monsieur, that you too would be taking your life in your hands if you followed in his footsteps."

Blake nodded his agreement.

"That is, no doubt, correct, monsieur," he said coolly. "On the other hand it would be by no means the first time I had done so. I agree with you that poor Coignet, in all probability, visited that house again last night and paid for it with his life. But I haven't the slightest intention of taking advantage of your offer to quit, monsieur. On the contrary, Coignet's murder but makes me keener than ever to get on the track of these criminals, and, with your permission, I propose losing no time in going through this dossier, after which I shall lay my plans.

"I have come across one or two things in Coignet's report that have interested me profoundly. I do not care, at this stage, to state what they are, but I want to examine them further. As soon as I have completed my study of the dossier I shall advise you what I propose doing as a beginning. That will be some time today. I take it that, as usual, when I am working in France you will see that I am provided with the necessary papers and authority in case of necessity —for my assistant as well."

"But yes, monsieur. I shall see that you are provided with the same papers which I myself would carry, and, of course, for your assistant too. And believe me, M. Blake, I am profoundly indebted to you for what you are doing for us. I feel confident that if these scoundrels are run to earth in the end we shall owe no small portion of the result to your distinguished counsel and assistance."

Blake made a deprecatory gesture and rose.

"I shall return to my hotel now, monsieur," he said. "I shall lose no time in examining this dossier, and I shall visit you again during the afternoon. When I come I shall inform you what I propose doing, and I should be glad if the necessary papers were ready, as I may wish to leave Paris this evening."

"That shall be done, M. Blake."

Blake shook hands with the Prefect, and with the bulky leather dossier under his arm, took his way out.

From the Ile de la Cite he took a taxi back to the Carlitz Hotel in the Rue de Rivoli where he was staying and where he found his young assistant, Tinker, waiting in the lounge for his return.

At a signal the lad rose, accompanied him up to the sitting-room of their suite, and before opening the dossier Blake gave the lad a brief resume of what the Prefect had told him, beginning at the first of the series of hold-ups and finishing with the news of the tragic death of Coignet of the Sûreté, which had come in over the telephone from Poissy while he was in conference with M. Dupuis.

Then he opened the dossier, and with Tinker at his elbow, pencil and notebook ready to jot down any comments Blake would utter as he went along, the examination proceeded.

They kept at it steadily until lunch-time, and immediately after resumed their labours, finally completing the work a few minutes before three o'clock. When he had scanned the several pages of notes which Tinker had jotted down Blake closed the dossiers and rose.

"Wait here," he said briefly. "I shall be back inside an hour."

That evening two strangers arrived at the town of Poissy on the Seine. They did not reach the place either together, or at the same time, and, certainly from the radical difference in the appearance of the two, no one would have suspected that they had even the slightest knowledge of each other.

The first to arrive came in a small two-seater car which he garaged at the Hotel L'Esturgeon, after which he entered the hotel to inquire if he could be given a room for a few days. He was, it appeared, a young Indian of the student type who, he announced in fair French, had heard of the fishing at Poissy and wished to try his luck during a brief vacation.

He wore a plain white turban, such as forms part of the dress of the banian or merchant class in India, but otherwise his garments were of European pattern. His skin was, of course, dark, and had one been able to see him stripped one would have seen that his whole body was of the same shade. He was received with a good deal more deference than would have been the case in either England or America, for our French neighbours have a radically different idea regarding the coloured and negro races than have we, and in France they are in every way socially accepted by the vast majority on an equality with themselves —a condition that applies to the yellow races as well.

It appeared that the visitor could be given the choice of three or four rooms, and having expressed a desire to have one, if possible, overlooking the river, he was conducted to the first floor, where he was shown a small room which looked out directly on the heavy glass roof of the hotel restaurant which is on the sheer bank of the river.

He did not commit himself to this, but asked if he could look at another, and when the proprietaire discovered that the visitor would not object to one on the second floor (which was also the top) he showed him a corner room in which one window looked out over the river directly opposite the house on the island mentioned by Sub-inspector Coignet in his report to the Sûreté, and the other on the strand, and from which, too, one could see straight into the windows of the small hotel facing the strand at which Coignet had stayed, known as the Rendezvous des Pecheurs.

It was not a large room but was clean and comfortable, and after a brief inspection the young Indian expressed his satisfaction with it.

That was about seven o'clock in the evening, and, as soon as his bags had been brought up, he got into a suit of baggy English flannels and descended to the veranda restaurant, for in that little place no one thought of getting into formal clothes for dinner.

His table, like his room, gave him a full view of the little island some hundred feet or so across the water from where he sat, and by choosing a chair from which he could look up stream instead of down, he could see everyone who crossed the bridge which was just above, and almost adjoining the upper wall of the hotel, and in some cases, could catch glimpses of people entering and leaving the house on the island as well as moving about under the trees at that place.

For any casual visitor to Poissy the room he had been given and the table he had selected gave a perfectly delightful view of one of the prettiest spits in the whole length of the Seine; to one who might, by some chance, have a particular interest in that end of the bridge, the little islands opposite the hotel and the house on the one which abutted against the fourth pier of the bridge, it would have been impossible to find two spots better situated from which one could keep a surveillance.

The second stranger to arrive came by train, but unlike the young Indian student who came from the direction of Paris the other individual came by train from farther down the river, in the direction of Villennes.

He was not of a type to be specially remarked upon in that part of France, for he was exactly similar in appearance to scores of persons who are to be seen all along the banks of the Seine in the summer as soon as the fishing season opens.

He was tall, of bulky build and displayed a ragged iron grey moustache and a not very well kept beard, also tinged with grey. He was dressed in a baggy grey suit that was none too clean, a blue checked shirt which was provided with a loose old collar of the same material, no tie. and a wide brimmed cheap straw-hat, which is known in some places as a "cow's breakfast."

He carried a cheap bamboo fishing rod, of the four joint take-down pattern, a dilapidated landing net, a brown canvas creel and a small leather bag that apparently held his personal belongings.

In each lapel of his coat could be seen fish-hooks of various sizes, some with bits of line still adhering to them. And if one stood close to him one could see that each bulging side pocket was also stuffed with fishing paraphernalia of various kinds.

In brief, he was of the type of ardent fisherman who simply exists through the dead months of the year, until the season opens, and then for him begins the halcyon days when he will angle for hours upon end, either from the bank or a punt hitched to a stake out where the current runs free, in pursuit of the elusive fish, and, whether his catch is large or small, meanders home at dusk with a soul full of contentment. They are to be found in every country under the sun, and in no place are they more ubiquitous than along the banks of the Seine in the months of the summer and early autumn.

Therefore the bulky person who carried his own kit down from the station created not a whit of curiosity among any of the inhabitants who saw him pass. Nor did he do so at the Rendezvous des Pecheurs, which catered firstly and foremost for just such as he.

He was obviously French, and one would gather from his accent that he was probably a native of Normandy.

In response to his inquiry he was informed that accommodation was available, and he indicated a desire to go up to his room at once. He was given the choice of two, and after some half-unintelligible grumbling, chose one on the first floor which looked out across the strand to the river, and beyond that to the two lower of the three islands which lay in the stream.

He wasted little time in cleaning himself, but, after depositing his bag and fishing-gear, descended to the small restaurant, and managed to get a table near the door from which he could command a view of the front and one side of the Hotel L'Esturgeon across the way, and the river, with just a bit of the island by the bridge showing.

Within half an hour of arriving at the little hotel he had succeeded in establishing an atmosphere of reserve about him, but in the bar, after he had dined, he was soon in conversation with the proprietaire —himself a keen angler —about the possibilities of the river at that time, and an argument as to the best form of bait to be used.

Like all such conversation, it eventually developed into a tongue-matching of fishing reminiscences, and continued until it was time for the patron to put up the shutters.

The newly arrived guest, before mounting to his room, announced that he might wish to go for a walk before turning in, and at that was given a key by which he could let himself in if he did so.

He did not go out just then, however, but on reaching his room, closed and locked the door after him, and, without turning on the light, drew up a chair to the open window.

It was a clear night outside, and by the light of a half-moon he could distinctly see the river beyond the trees on the strand, and again the heavy bulk of the foliage on the islands.

Just above he could make out the straight lines of the upper portion of the bridge, and a little distance out a light among the trees, which he knew must come from the house on the island which abutted on to the bridge.

Then he brought his gaze round to the other hotel opposite him, and for some minutes he studied the place in silence, taking particular note of the front and side rooms and the two on the corner which would command a view of both the strand and the river.

The place seemed very quiet, for beyond a light in under the veranda, there was no other gleam of illumination in the whole building, and it would seem that all the occupants had gone to bed.

But had he taken up his position at his window half an hour sooner, he would have caught the fugitive gleam of a flashlight in the second floor corner room, a gleam that came and went intermittently, and which had been visible from only a small radius of area in which had been included the small hotel where the fisherman was staying. But he had missed that, and he did not know that the young Indian student who had taken up his quarters at the other hotel had been sitting at the window of the other room until certain events which he had noticed caused him to desert his post, and follow a very peculiar programme for a stranger to the place.

After dining in the veranda restaurant, the young Indian had gone to his room, and there had carefully locked the door after him.

Next he had opened the shutters of both windows, and for a little while had stood gazing down at the moonlit water beneath. Just at the corner of the building, and so old and big that its spreading branches spread well round each side and far out over the glass veranda top of the restaurant, was a beautiful chestnut-tree, around which the roof of the veranda had been built.

Just in front of the two windows of the room occupied by the young Indian student the branches had been cut away to permit a view of the river and the islands, as well as the strand and a portion of the street opposite.

The young man seemed quite engrossed in his contemplation of this tree, for he did not move for several minutes.

Then he approached the other window and gazed across at the smaller hotel. Through the open door he could see directly into the bar, and among those there he could make out the figure of the bulky fisherman who had just finished his dinner and was fraternising with the landlord.

He withdrew from the window after a brief survey of the place, and with some need for caution placed a chair in the corner of the room just between the two windows, which were so close that the two

34

swing halves of the open french sashes almost touched.

Next he opened one of his bags, and after a brief search, took out a small self-generating electric torch and a small but powerful pair of night-glasses. Equipped with these, he took up his post on the chair between the two windows, from which position he could command an uninterrupted view of the first four spans of the bridge, the island which abutted against the fourth span, the house on the island where Coignet of the Paris Sûreté had had his strange experience the night before he had been foully murdered, the narrow stretch of calm water that lay between the hotel and the island, and, through the window, the little hotel known as the Rendezvous des Pecheurs.

For nearly two hours he sat there focussing most of his attention upon the little island where stood the house of mystery, but occasionally turning his gaze in the direction of the hotel on the opposite side of the strand, and now and then flashing a beam from his electric torch in that direction.

Thus he sat, and thus he intended to sit until some answering message came from the other hotel. But when the second hour had almost run its course he suddenly sat up and gave all his attention to the island by the bridge, for at that moment something had occurred which roused his acute interest and curiosity.

TINKER, for the young "Indian student" was Blake's assistant, and none other, was gazing through the night-glasses when, on the narrow stretch of silvery water, a small canoe glided noiselessly into view.

In it was a single individual, who was wielding a double-bladed paddle with so much skill that the surface of the water was scarcely rippled where the spoon dipped in and out.

For a few seconds the little craft glided along under his vision, and then it passed into the heavy shadow cast by the dense overhanging trees on the little island by the bridge.

From where he sat Tinker could just see a strip of light between the third and fourth piers of the bridge, and he watched that to see if the canoe would pass through on its way up-stream. But it did not reappear again, and, at the end of a few minutes, he knew that it must have nosed into the bank under the trees.

Although he had only been in Poissy a couple of hours or so, he knew there was nothing out of the way in a boat stopping at the island, for he had seen from the veranda of his hotel a small landing at the lower end of the island at which half a dozen punts and other river craft had been moored. While he dined he had seen men enter them and row off, and also seen others arrive bearing passengers.

It was plain that a considerable number of customers of the house on the island arrived in that way, and were probably folk who lived either below or above Poissy, or across on the other side of the river.

But there had been nothing secretive in the movements of those craft. They had arrived quite openly, and their occupants had made no effort to hide the purpose of their coming.

In an idle way, during dinner, Tinker had questioned the old waiter who served him, and picked up quite a little fund of information. The old man, who had served at L'Esturgeon for many years, had nothing good to say about the place on the island, but, on the other hand, he made no definite statements against those who lived there, held back, Tinker opined, by fear.

Tinker made no mention of the body that had been found in the river that same morning, but, along towards the end of the meal, the old man himself raised the item of news as something that might interest the visitor, and from what he said Tinker gathered that while it was accepted as being a murder, there was, so far, no suspicion among the ordinary inhabitants against anyone at the house on the island.

That was about the gist of what he gathered while he ate and watched the movements on the river. And it was because of this that he had already learned, he was more than usually interested in the very quiet way in which the small canoe had slipped into the shadow under the trees opposite him.

He dropped to his knees, and resting the glasses on the window-sill trained them on the spot about where he thought the canoe must have touched the bank. He could make out nothing at first, but then, suddenly, he saw the little craft distinctly as she rode light and high against the revettment, just a few feet from where it touched the stone of the bridge pier.

At that side of the house he could also see a half-open door, and this, he fancied, must be the one spoken of by poor Coignet in his report to the Prefect.

He kept the glasses moving from the point where the canoe lay along a line that ran from it to the door through which the light shone, but though he was certain he was missing nothing that passed there, he saw not a single sign of the solitary occupant of the canoe. Which in a way was a little strange, for if the fellow hadn't landed in order to go up to the house for a drink, what was he doing?

It was then his unspoken question received a strange answer, for just beside the canoe he saw the gleam of something white. It seemed to move and dip and waver as he looked at it, and he was deeply puzzled as to what was happening.

Then the lifting moon seemed to cast a brighter glow across the water, or else his eyes were growing more accustomed to the gloom, for all at once it came to him what was going on.

"It's a man stripping," he thought. "It's probably the same bird who came in the canoe, and that white patch is the upper part of his body or else his undervest. There it is lower down now —his legs. That's it as sure as anything, he is stripping. But why is he being so darned secret about it? There are lots of places along here where he could go in for a dip if he wanted to, and no one would say anything. Perhaps he hasn't any swimming trunks along with him, and wants a quiet spot. Well, I don't blame him. I wouldn't mind a dip myself. But there, what is that? He's putting something on. The lower part of his body is covered, and now most of the upper part. It's a swimming suit —that's what it is, so he isn't unprovided after all. Then why the jolly old secrecy? Does he favour that spot more than any other, and is he afraid of the old pirate who owns the house there? If not, why?"

Tinker continued to watch, and as, for a brief moment, the person under survey paused on the sheer edge of the revetment, and a swaying branch allowed the moonlight to fall full upon him. Tinker could see plainly that he was dressed for swimming, and, to all intents and purposes, was preparing to go into the water.

And he did go in. He bent down, and gripping the edge of the revetment with his hands, turned round and slipped down as smoothly and with as little noise as a water rat.

By gazing intently, Tinker managed to see that he hung there for a few seconds, then his head disappeared, and all that the watching lad could tell about his movements was the series of small ripples that came dancing out from the shadow into the moonlight.

And though he waited and watched every portion of the revetment, from the stone pier of the bridge to the lower point of the island, he saw not another sign of the other, nor of any more ripples. From the moment when he had allowed his body to slip into the water, he had disappeared as completely as if he had gone to the bottom like a stone.

It was more than puzzling —it was distinctly intriguing. What had become of the fellow? Tinker asked himself as he swept the edge of the revetment with the glasses.

He had certainly gone into the water. There could be no mistake about that. The ripples were proof that nothing could hide. And no man living could swim in that calm water without making a wake, be it ever so faint, that would not show on the moonlit surface. A rat would have left a distinct trail.

But there was nothing, not a breath on the surface, not the faintest hint of a splash on the still night air. It wasn't a suicide. No one ever drowned like that. Even if a man had tied a hundred pound weight to his feet he would have made more ripples than had shown, and certainly there would have been air bubbles, too, which would have come to the surface and shown against that glassy face.

Then, also, a person intending to commit suicide did not usually go to the trouble of stripping and donning a swimming suit. But as sure as guns someone —a man —had entered the water at that place and had disappeared as completely as could be conceived.

Tinker took occasion, while he puzzled over the mystery, to flash another cautious signal in the direction of the hotel across the way, but when no answer came he turned back to his contemplation of the island.

He was just in time to see the second of the queer happenings which were to make that night one of deep mystery. In this instance he saw the silhouette of a figure on the bridge. The man —for he was certain it was a man —had evidently come along the approach on the Poissy side, and had walked out towards the fourth span where steps led down into the front portion of the garden belonging to the house on the island.

Tinker gave half his attention to this individual the while he also kept up a surveillance of the spot where the first man had disappeared.

He saw the second person pause on the bridge and appear to look in either direction. Then he came close to the low rail on the lower side of the bridge and seemed to lean over.

As far as Tinker could see, watching him where he stood full in the moonlight, he was wearing an overcoat of some dark material, and the next instant he gave a gasp as he found that not only was this so, but that underneath it he was wearing a swimming suit!

The man on the bridge swept off the long coat at a single stroke, and Tinker saw him lean out over the rail, swing it out and downwards so that it fell among the bushes beneath, close to the stone pier of the bridge, and not half a dozen feet from where the canoe lay tied.

Following that, the man swung lightly over the rail, and slid down until his toes were touching the out-sloping buttress beneath him. There was no difficulty of a toe-hold there, for the stonework was hundreds of years old, with the upper part thickly moss and bush grown, while, beneath, the jointure of the stones was chipped and broken.

An active man could climb either up or down with ease. And the man Tinker was watching went down as lightly as a monkey, until he was standing on a narrow stone curbing that formed the normal water-mark of the river. Tinker saw him pause there for just a moment or two —saw him twist round a little, then he slid into the water, and in four or five strokes had passed into the shadow of the trees close to where the empty canoe lay tied.

From beneath the trees the ripples of his wake continued to come for a few seconds, and then they ceased —abruptly, entirely as if an invisible hand had wiped the glassy surface of the water clean. He had disappeared as utterly and in as mystifying a manner as the one who had come in the canoe!

Tinker was dumbfounded.

"I'm not crazy," he muttered, "and all I've had to drink is a single glass of French beer that wouldn't turn the head of a six months' old baby. And I'm equally certain my eyes are not playing me tricks. Then, what does it mean? That man who came in the canoe went into the water by the bank there and immediately disappeared. As far as I have been able to see he hasn't come to the surface yet. Then along comes another bird, and after chucking his coat down by the canoe, comes down that old pier like a squirrel, and swims into the same spot, where he, too, vanishes. And he hasn't come up again, either! More than that, his ripples have all vanished!

"It looks as if Coignet was right when he said in his report that, in his opinion, the house on that island would bear investigation by the local police, aside from the business that took him there. Those two men didn't commit suicide, and as they are not any more amphibian than I am, they must have gone somewhere! And —Hallo, though, look who's here! Someone coming from the house —perhaps to investigate! Now perhaps we shall see some fun!"

He watched the figure that had emerged from the side door just then, and saw that it was a man walking towards the spot where the canoe lay. He moved silently, and as one familiar with his surroundings, but, as far as Tinker could see, with no particular care to keep his movements secret, which made the lad think it must be someone belonging to the house. He came on until, for a moment, he was lost in the shadow, but then he reappeared again, and Tinker could see him standing close to the nose of the canoe. He stood thus for a few seconds gazing down, apparently into the water.

Tinker was wondering if he were puzzled over the presence of the canoe there, and he could not understand why the pile of garments left by the first man on the edge of the bank did not attract his attention. But he soon saw the reason why they didn't, for suddenly the man began to disrobe just as Tinker had seen the other strip.

He watched him until the white of his torso showed, then he

could see it disappear as the man drew on a garment which Tinker didn't need to see more closely to know was a swimming suit.

Then his movements were an exact repetition of those of the one who had arrived in the canoe. In fact it might have been the same person for all the difference there was. He slid over the edge of the revetment and into the water as smoothly as an otter. He held thus for a moment or so, then he let go and —disappeared.

From under the trees a few baby ripples swept out across the mirrored surface, then they ended abruptly.

Tinker laid the glasses down, flashed a signal across to the other hotel, saw that it remained unanswered, then leant against the window guard rail with his eyes fixed on the spot where, unless he had suddenly taken leave of his senses, he was prepared to swear he had just seen three men, one after the other, slip into the water and vanish utterly from the scheme of things.

It was uncanny the sinister silence of it all. It was unreal to watch the unrolling of that silent drama in the pool of shadows beneath the trees. It was like a fleeting vision into some dark glass where the powers of darkness are employed in some secret rite —like a film that has snapped at some critical point, with the whole picture vanishing from the screen as if it never had had existence.

For the better part of half an hour Tinker divided his attention between the island and the window of the small hotel opposite.

Had he known that the rather dirty-looking bulky fisherman who had arrived that evening and whom he had glimpsed in the bar a little while before was Sexton Blake, he would simply have sat tight and waited until he got an answer to the signal agreed upon before they parted in Paris, Tinker to motor direct to Poissy, and Blake to go by rail to a town farther down the river, and from which he would make his first assault, so to say.

But other than knowing that Blake intended adopting the guise of a fisherman of the country, he did not know what his exact appearance would be, and certainly there had been no suggestion of the clean-cut figure of his master in the hulking native he had seen in conversation with the landlord across the street.

Therefore, he took it that something had come up to detain Blake, and that if he did not reach Poissy by one of the later trains that night, he would not show up until the following morning.

"He doesn't look like turning up now," he muttered. "It is after eleven o'clock, and, with the exception of that bar across the road and the house on the island, the whole place seems to be asleep. I haven't heard a sound here in the hotel for more than an hour. I wish they hadn't closed the door of that bar at the Rendezvous des Pecheurs. If it was open I could see when the guv'nor turned up. There is someone in there still, all right, for it is lighted up. But that business over at the island is certainly queer. I don't know what is up, but my orders are to keep a sharp eye on the island and the house —on everyone who goes to the place and leaves it, and to investigate as far as possible anything that looks suspicious.

"Well, I fancy what I have seen to-night could be called suspicious all right, and unless I am very greatly mistaken it will bear a little investigation. At any rate, I am going to take a chance on it unless those three mermen reappear before I can get there. I'll fix myself so I'll also be a pretty good imitation of a seal, and it is a lucky thing this black stain won't come off in ordinary water, for I'll have to swim for it."

With that, Tinker laid the torch and glasses aside and stood up. He took off the turban which he had kept on until then, and slipped quickly out of his clothes.

In the dusk of the room his darkly-stained body scarcely showed, and as he glanced down at himself he again thanked his luck that he had chosen that disguise. From one of his bags he took a small pair of bathing trunks —just tights without a tunic —and got into these. Next he poked about in a smaller bag, without which he rarely travelled on a case, and after a few moment's search, brought out a large bottle.

He took this over near the window and removed the cork. Then he poured a little of the contents into his hand and began to smear his body with it. He kept on pouring out small portions of the thick liquid and rubbing it on until he had covered every particle of his body, with the exception of the loins which were covered with the trunks. And when he had finished he was as thickly greased from head to foot as any Thursday Island diver who ever slipped into the China Straits in search of oyster shell.

He re-corked the bottle and returned it to the small bag which he carefully locked. He also secured the other bags and dropped the bunch of keys into a small pocket which had been fashioned inside the swimming trunks.

Then he made sure that the door was well fastened, after which he again approached the window which looked out on the river, and stood gazing across at the spot near where the canoe lay tied. It was as still as before, and with a little grunt Tinker climbed on to the sill.

Holding the side of the window with one hand, he swung outwards until his free hand could grasp one of the upper branches of the giant chestnut. His fingers curled round it, and the next moment he swung out lightly, catching hold with his other hand and giving his body easily as the branch dipped down under his weight.

He waited until its natural resiliency gave it a return spring, then he worked his way along through the branches above the glass top of the veranda restaurant —which was then just beneath him, and steadily downwards at the same time, until by the time he had covered the width of the glass roof he was close to the outer edge of it.

Just there a single branch of the chestnut poked out over the small pontoon float, at the foot of the steps leading from the hotel down to it. Tinker worked his way along this branch, the green wood bending a little more and a little more as he approached the end.

By the time he was within a couple of yards of it he could look down and see the smooth water directly underneath him. He hung there for a few seconds until the branch steadied a little, then he hung to the full extremity of his arms, brought his legs tight together, toes pointing downwards and let go gently.

He dropped, straight as an arrow, into the water beneath, his down-pointing toes cutting the surface and his oiled body slipping after, with scarcely a sound. His head disappeared, and the moment he was under water, he turned over and began swimming towards the island, some hundred feet or so distant. He came to the surface a few seconds later, and behind him was a shallow wake as he proceeded as sinuously as an eel.

The oiled body was, of course, an asset, and, but for the black crown of his head on the surface, it would have been next to impossible for a person standing even as close as on the hotel veranda to guess that someone was swimming across the moonlit stretch of water.

Thus he went for ever so brief a time; then he passed into the shadow of the trees which overhung the bank. Gradually the ripples caused by his passage wore away, and then it seemed, for the fourth time that night, that a swimmer had vanished in that pool of sinister shadow!

CHAPTER 7. The Watcher on the Bridge —Seen by the Three Musketeers —A Swim for Life.

TINKER clung to the edge of the bank with his fingers, the whole of his body submerged to the neck. He held himself as motionless as possible and, with his dark skin, it was impossible to see him from even a few feet away. Just on his left was the canoe, moving slightly back and forth under the impulse of some vagrant current.

Almost directly in front of him, on the bank, were two piles of garments, or what he took to be that, proving that what he had seen had been no figment of a moon-inspired imagination.

The canoe and clothes were tangible enough, and he was still convinced that everything else he had seen had occurred just as his eyes had visualised it.

After hanging motionless, watchful and waiting, for some little time he shifted his position with infinite caution and, while he explored beneath the water with his toes, worked his way along inch by inch towards the stone pier of the bridge, which loomed up darkly just a few feet away from him. It was somewhere there, he suspected, that the solution of the puzzle should be found.

He was just on the point of letting go and pushing across to the pier when he held himself rigid, listening. He had heard something above him, and now he could make out the sound of a steady footfall as someone came across the bridge.

He strained back and looked up, but could not see the person. Still he waited until the footsteps were directly above him and had passed on. They then came to a sudden pause, and a faint creaking sound followed. Then there was a ring of iron-shod heels as the person above descended the steps that led down to the house on the island.

"Someone going to that bar," thought Tinker, and a second later, as he heard the crunching of gravel and the bang of a door he knew he was right. But he did not guess for a moment that the man who had just walked along overhead was the same bulky-looking fisherman who had arrived at the Rendezvous des Pecheurs that evening.

As it grew quiet again Tinker let his fingers slip, and, with a slight kick against the revetment, sent himself across the water level kerbing of the stone pier. He clung here for a few moments, feeling about the triangular point of the buttress for finger and toe hold.

He discovered that the old stones had many crevices between them, and by a little active work he managed to climb up until he was standing on the kerbing, his fingers sunk into a crack between two of the stones and his body pressed flat against it.

Where he clung the shadow of the buttress itself effectually concealed him, and, even if one had looked down from directly above, it would have been difficult to pick him out.

From this position of slight elevation above the surface of the water it was possible, too, for him to see along the path towards the side door of the house on the island.

Five minutes, ten minutes dragged by, and then Tinker heard another slam, followed by a crunching of boot heels on gravel, as someone came out of the house and walked towards the iron steps leading up to the bridge.

He heard the ring of the iron-shod heels, and the faint creak of the gate at the top, then once more the measured pace above as the person, whoever it was, walked towards the Poissy side.

Tinker flattened himself like a limpet against the stone, thinking that it must be the same person who had gone into the place a little while before. He figured it must be just some casual customer who might not even glance down over the guard rail, but, even so, he was taking no chances. But when the pedestrian was directly above him, something happened that brought every nerve of the lad's on the qui vive, and banished from his mind all thought of the one above.

It came with such startling suddenness that he emitted an involuntary gasp for, close to the spot as he now was, the shock of it was far greater than when he had watched a similar phenomenon from the window of his room a hundred feet distant.

At one moment the water at his feet was as smooth and unruffled as a sheet of glass. The next the surface was broken abruptly as a head shot up into view. Part of a pair of white shoulders followed, and Tinker saw the arms flash against the dark of the water, as the apparition from the depths stroked in to the bank under the trees.

Scarcely had his fingers gripped the edge of the revetment than, at almost the same spot, another head appeared, and the owner followed the first one to the revetment.

Then for a third time Tinker saw a repetition of the phenomenon and, as all three clung to the edge, he tried to flatten himself still more against the stone. He clung, scarcely breathing, watching while first one, then the second, and the third crawled up on the bank and squatted on his haunches and, it seemed to the lad, gazed directly at him!

His mind was working swiftly. He had come across the narrow stretch of water in pursuit of a mystery. He had suspected that somewhere near the base of the great stone pier he could find a solution to it.

And, while he had not found a full answer to the puzzle, he had proved himself right in his belief that he had actually seen three human beings slip into the water in that pool of shadow, and not come up again until just then, when they had given him no little shock by the suddenness of their reappearance.

Now Tinker knew perfectly well that the outside limit for a man to remain under water is something in the neighbourhood of three minutes, and at that only the most seasoned of pearl divers can stand such length of pressure on lungs and ears. But unless he were stark mad, then he could only believe that those three individuals had gone under, and had remained under for more than half an hour.

At least they had certainly disappeared beneath the surface, close to where he was clinging, and they had reappeared at the same spot. And now he was stuck there like a barnacle waiting to see what would happen next.

He didn't have long to wait. He had had an uneasy feeling that eyes in the shadow had seen him and were watching him! Despite himself, he felt his skin begin to prickle as the skin nerves pulsed into goose-flesh. For a second a sharp wave of panic went over him, and then with a jerk he pulled himself together.

Nevertheless there was something uncanny about the whole business, and it was not lessened by the thought that those three mysterious creatures, who had exhibited all the qualities of amphibians from Mars, or some other distant sphere, were squatting there like three profane ghouls watching him with unblinking gaze. He knew that his nerve would stand just so much of that sort of strain. If something tangible, something earthly material did not happen soon he knew he would have to break it himself.

But it did happen, and it came as abruptly as those three heads had appeared from the smooth depths. Tinker could not have stated definitely that there had been any spoken word among the three opposite him. But he felt that in some way a message had been exchanged between them. Some instinct warned him to hold himself ready for "something," and he was as taut as a bowstring when, with no more warning than that occult warning which he had "felt" across the strip of water, Tinker saw them lurch over, and dive in with one accord.

But this time they did not disappear from view. On the contrary. They came straight for the stone pier where he clung, and as they came out of the shadow he saw, as the moonlight struck their eyes, that they were bent on murder —if they got him!

And he saw something else, too, for in that brief glance he realised, with an internal upheaval, that he had seen all three before.

Tinker poised himself and waited until they had almost reached the narrow kerbing on which he stood. He measured his chances with practised eye, and then, as a pair of hands reached up towards the kerbing, he flexed one knee and jammed his heel outward and downward with all his strength. It caught the nearest assailant full in the face, and sent him back with a grunt.

Tinker repeated the blow on the second, and then perforce took to the water in a clean dive that carried him completely over their heads. As he struck the water he began swimming with a quick crawl, but as his body slithered ahead he felt a pair of arms grip him about the thighs.

He wormed round, and struck back with his heels. The arms slipped, gripped again, slipped, then fingers plucked futilely at him as he made a desperate effort and broke clear. But it wasn't to the power of his heels that Tinker owed that temporary advantage. Rather was it to the oil which he had rubbed on his limbs before taking to the water, and which made his body as difficult to hold as that of any greased savage.

For the moment Tinker had a slight lead, but as he rolled over to a strong side stroke he saw that all three were after him. He saw, too, up on the bridge that some pedestrian near the end by the buildings must have heard the racket beneath, for a figure was silhouetted against the sky as he bent curiously over to see what was going on.

Instinctively he kept away from the float at the foot of the stone steps leading down from the hotel. So far he had one distinct advantage over his pursuers. He knew for positive fact the identity of each one of the three, and, in that disguise of his, they could not possibly have recognised him. Which Tinker wanted less than anything in the world at that moment.

He had recognised them. Even as he slithered along through the water at his best burst of speed, the thought was throbbing in his mind. He had recognised them! And in that one flash of recognition a whole page of what he and Blake were up against unfolded itself before him.

At first, when he had seen the mysterious actions of first one, then another, and still another, across at the edge of the island, he had followed it up simply in obedience to orders. Those orders had been to keep a sharp look-out, and in case he saw anything out of the ordinary in connection with the island, or the house on it, to investigate it.

He did so, and now he had uncovered far more than he had ever dreamed of doing when he had greased his body and swung off the outreaching branch of the giant chestnut into the river.

That moment of recognition not only made him determined to get away, to escape seizure and a similar fate to that which had overtaken poor Coignet of the Sûreté (for he was dead certain he knew now how the sub-inspector had died), but he wanted to get in touch with Blake at the earliest possible moment.

Blake must know this which he had to tell him. Blake must be put in possession of the startling discovery he had made without delay, for, as he swam along with those three menacing figures sliding through the water after him —more menacing and more deadly than sharks through their sinister lack of outcry —he knew he was the only being on the side of law, at that moment, who could name the three bandits who had committed the series of killings and robberies which had so stirred the Paris Prefecture, and whose latest victim had been Coignet.

The only person who could name them, and he wanted to whisper just three words in Blake's ears. Those words were: "The Three Musketeers"! And if he had only known that the figure silhouetted on the bridge at that very moment was none other than Blake's, he would have set himself a very different course through the water.

But he did not know, so, as he came to the end of the little island which abutted on to the fourth span of the bridge, he saw the narrow channel of water which separated it from the other two just below it; he took a sharp turn to the right, and the next second both he and his pursuers had disappeared from the view of the watcher on the bridge —a very puzzled watcher he was, too, for it was impossible for Sexton Blake to see exactly what had transpired, or to know whether the four swimming units were local youths out for a night lark, or if they had been on the island.

Tinker held his lead round the end of the island and past the tip of the first of the two below.

Then he felt a strong undertow as he came to the channel which separated the two lower ones, and the next second found himself in a miniature maelstrom formed just at the tip of the outer and larger island by the conjunction of the main current of the river with the two narrow channels separating the three islands.

He knew as he struck the swirl that it would be fatal to remain in it. Already two of his pursuers were almost upon him, while the third was only a yard behind them. Before he could get through the swirl into the smoother, but faster, water beyond, they would have him, and, surrounded there, the oil upon his body would not save him a second time.

It might be that they were only curious to find out who it was that had been lurking by the pier. They must have seen that he was apparently a black-skinned person, but Tinker knew if they dragged him ashore to examine him (presuming they did not just push him under, and keep him under until he was drowned, a thing of which the Three Musketeers were quite capable), they must soon discover his identity; and once they knew that it was a quick step to guessing the truth.

Even if they did not know just why he was in Poissy in such disguise, they would kill him out of hand in any event, for the Three Musketeers had a long score marked up against Sexton Blake and Tinker.

To go back was equally out of the question. Such a move would bring him into the midst of them. Again, they were now between him and the smaller of the two islands, and, in any case, it would not have been large enough to give him any concealment. They would have been too close after him to risk landing there.

He might succeed in a dash upstream to the right, and land on the upper island where the house of mystery stood, but that would only be out of the frying-pan into the fire. Coignet had paid with his life for trusting himself on that spot.

There was left, then, just one move other than to try and get through the swirl to the main river just ahead. That was to give himself to the sweep of the current and try to land on the point of the larger and outer island.

From his conversation with Emile, the old waiter at his hotel, he knew that the greater part of this outer island was the property of the hotel, and knew further that, before the war, when things round Poissy had been more prosperous, it had formed a sort of annex where visitors could sit under the trees or promenade along pretty little wooded paths. But during and since the war it had been little used, and, according to what he had heard, had become almost overgrown with shrubs and bushes.

From the veranda cafe of the hotel he had seen some dilapidated steps at the point near where he was now fighting the miniature maelstrom, and as he made his decision to take that course in preference to the other single alternative, he swung round and threw himself forward with the current.

Faster even than he had hoped, he was swept down upon the point. He bumped twice against submerged posts which he had been unable to see, but the next moment his fingers touched the edge of the lower steps, and even as his two leading pursuers swung after him he drew up his knee and crawled out.

He turned and reached down. Under his grasp some of the rotten wood of the old water-logged steps came away easily enough, and just as the pair shot out their hands to grip the edge, Tinker brought his improvised club down full and hard upon a head he knew belonged to the member of the trio known as Algy Somerton.

Then he struck again with even greater force, and as the strip of wood crashed on to Archie Pherison's skull it broke into pieces.

The third, Reggie Fetherston, had caught the edge of the steps a little lower down, and was already drawing himself out of the water. Tinker made a frantic effort to tear off another strip of wood, succeeded in getting hold of a short piece, which he hurled with all his force full into Fetherston's face, sending the latter back into the water with a violent curse.

Then Tinker stumbled up the steps and, trusting to blind luck, tore off along a path which seemed to lead towards the other end, or other side, of the island, he could not tell which. But even as he ran he knew that his pursuers had also gained the bank and were after him!

TINKER knew nothing of the island on which he had landed other than what he had learned from old Emile, the garcon at his hotel, and a fairly ancient picture on the menu-card there, which had apparently been reproduced from a photograph taken back some forty or fifty years before.

From these two sources he knew that there should be a promenade path running right round the island, but he remembered that the waiter had mentioned that since the war, when the popularity of the place had declined, the heavy bushes on the island had gained headway, and it took his naked limbs and torso just about ten seconds to discover that this was indeed so, and that the variety which had proved most prolific was of the thorny type.

From the top of the dilapidated steps, where he had landed, he plunged off to the left, and, from the feel of gravel under his feet, knew that he had struck the old path. On either side thorny bushes hung in close, digging into his flesh and sweeping the skin painfully as he forced his way along.

He knew from the sounds behind that his three pursuers had also landed, and he found a grain of consolation in the thought that, if they followed him, they would suffer as much from the bushes as did he.

He lost the path repeatedly, dashing blindly into half-wild roses and briars, but he kept on, despite the scores of small wounds which had been inflicted, for he knew they were as nothing to what would be his portion if he fell into the hands of the ruthless trio behind. What had happened to poor Coignet was enough to keep that in the forefront of his mind.

And then, all of a sudden, the path seemed to open out. A faint gleam of moonlight filtered through the trees overhead, and a light stirring of a new-born night breeze sent the towering poplars swaying gracefully. He felt soft turf under his feet, and the next instant crashed full tilt into a wire-netting fence.

He swung to the right, and gave an involuntary grunt of pain as he crashed into an obstacle directly in his path, and, as he shot headlong over it, made out that it was a wheelbarrow, left there he couldn't tell how many years before. He got to his knees, and then his feet. He started on again, and took the risk of crossing a small, open

51

place.

In the shadow of the trees beyond he came upon the gaping entrance of a small gardener's shed of sorts, and he recalled then what the garcon had told him about the island still being used as a vegetable garden for the hotel.

He hesitated and listened. At that moment no sounds of pursuit reached him, and the next instant he had plunged into the gloom of the shed. He found some dried grass in one corner, and, after lifting it up, threw himself down. Then he lay, listening intently.

He was thinking that the briar-choked path had daunted the ardour of his pursuers and had driven them back. Certainly, the passage had been painful enough to make it unattractive to anyone, clad as he and they were, except under the greatest duress.

So far, Tinker felt positive, the Three Musketeers could not have the faintest suspicion of the strange figure they had surprised clinging to the kerbing of the great stone pier of the bridge. That is to say, they could not guess that it was he, Tinker, or that he and Sexton Blake were in Poissy.

On the other hand, he knew, beyond the shadow of a doubt, that the three were Archie Pherison, Algy Somerton, and Reggie Fetherston, known commonly in the criminal and police circles of half a dozen countries as the Three Musketeers.

It is true there was nothing actual to connect the series of outrages that had occurred in Paris and the neighbourhood of that city with that trio; nor was there any sort of proof to say that they had had anything to do with the brutal murder of Coignet, of the Paris Prefecture.

On the other hand, there was the fact that three bandits had been connected with the series of outrages, and there was what Coignet had written in his report, and which he had managed to get through to headquarters before being murdered. The whole affair was of the sort that would appeal to the criminal instincts of the Three Musketeers.

Robbery with violence —cold-blooded murder —ruthless crime in all its phases —all these fitted in with what he himself knew of the Three Musketeers, despite their somewhat vapid, monocled appearance and the silly mannerisms which had stamped them as three aimless, good-for-nothings about the West End of London. Then there was the strange occurrence of that very evening —an occurrence that had taken place at the same spot where the trail picked up by

Coignet had ended, just as the detective's life had ended.

Even if the Three Musketeers had had no hand in the recent series of outrages, it was pretty good betting, Tinker knew, that they could be up to no good. Honest men don't act as he had seen the Three Musketeers act. What had become of them when they had disappeared, one after another, beneath the surface of the water, he couldn't even attempt to guess.

But if he got away that night with his life, he was determined that he —and, of course, Blake —would find out the answer to the riddle before they left Poissy. But just then the great problem was to get away.

Something of the above was running through his mind while he lay crouching in the corner of the old shed on the island. For a time he heard nothing but the faint sweep of the poplars overhead, as the night breeze stirred them.

Then from a distance, either up or down river, came the steady chug-chug of a power-lighter making its way against the current, and, following that, there came the rumble and roar of an express train as it swept through the town.

Tinker could have heard nothing in his immediate neighbourhood while the train was rushing through, but when the rumble died away, he suddenly became acutely aware of the sound of low voices close to him. And they were speaking in English.

"I tell you I know he came this way," one voice was saying. "I distinctly saw him cross this patch of open ground. He seemed to dash through under the trees then. But he can't get away on the outside of the island. The current is too strong, and the river too wide, for him to make the opposite bank."

"Well, then, he will have to come back this way or make for the upper end, where he landed," said the second voice. "If he does the first we shall catch him here, and, if he does the second, Algy will nab him by the steps. I don't see why we make all this fuss over him, anyway. These blamed thorns have scratched me from head to foot. What will we do with him when we get him?"

"That remains to be seen," responded the first voice, which Tinker could now distinguish as belonging to Archie Pherison, the one who was probably the leader of the trio, if leader there was. "There is something darned queer about finding a nigger on that pier just as we came to the surface. Don't forget that it is only two days since that meddler from the Sûreté turned up here. The prefect is not going to let that pass without a pretty thorough investigation. And that is why I want to get my hands on that coon. If he is just a stray nigger we scared, then it is all right. But it may be someone else."

"It strikes me we ought to be clearing out of here if that is the case," remarked the first voice, after a pause. "We are about ready to do so, and a delay may be dangerous."

"Two days yet, and we will do so," answered Pherison. "But there are things to be done. We haven't finished our business with old Wertheim, and we can't go until we do. Besides, the Sultan won't reach Havre for another three days. And, anyway, I don't know that we won't pull off another stunt before we go. I'd give something to tickle up the prefect just once more."

Silence fell again then, and crouching still lower, Tinker pondered on what he had just heard. He knew now, beyond the shadow of a doubt, that the Three Musketeers were up to, and had been up to, nefarious work of some sort, and it was plain that somewhere at Poissy they had a lair.

What business it was they had to finish up before clearing out, he didn't know, but their mention of the "meddler from the Sûreté," was enough to tell him now how poor Coignet had met his death.

Nor was that all. Some persons, overhearing the conversation, would have been puzzled at Pherison's remarks about the "Sultan not reaching Havre for another three days." But those words told Tinker a lot. They did not refer to any person who was a sultan, but, he knew, could only mean the private steam-yacht Sultan, property of Mathew Cardolak, the strange, eccentric multi-millionaire, who lived in America, and for whom the Three Musketeers had carried out many a coup in the past.

If the Sultan was coming to France it could only be to pick up the three crooks, which meant that either they had been employed on some mission for Cardolak or were about to embark on one for him.

Swiftly Tinker thought that there was very little about the recent outrages in Paris and the vicinity that seemed the type of thing to be inspired by Mathew Cardolak. They had all been sheer banditry for monetary —or the equivalent —gain. That, he knew, held no appeal for the multi-millionaire, who already had untold wealth.

If there had been any rare antique connected with the outrages it would have been easier to connect Cardolak with them. But in those few minutes he had gathered a good deal of priceless information, and he was more determined than ever that they should not get their hands on him.

They believed him to be still on the island —which was true. They did not know at just what point he was lurking, however, while, from what he heard, he knew that Fetherston and Pherison were close by the shed in which he lay concealed, while Algy Somerton was keeping watch at the other end near the steps where he had landed.

There was a slight advantage in that, but it remained to be seen if he would be able to turn it to any use. He didn't have to wait long to find out, for even while he debated the point, he heard Reggie Fetherston speak again, and his heart gave a sudden leap to his throat as the bandit drawled:

"My word, Archie, old man, I hadn't noticed that before. I think I'll just dig about inside. I thought the opening to that old shed was just a shadow hole under the trees. Perhaps our darkie friend has been there all the time, listening to what we have been saying. You wait here, and if I flush him, be ready to snaffle him."

They must spot him now. Tinker knew that without any further telling. If they cornered him in the old shed he wouldn't have the vestige of a chance to escape.

He shifted his position with infinite caution, and raised himself on one knee. There came no sound of movement from the outside, but suddenly the opening became blurred at one side, and he knew that one of the pair was coming in.

Then the silhouette blended with the wall on his right, and now he could hear a low, brushing sort of sound as the intruder crept along towards the back of the shed.

Still Tinker waited. Judging from what he had heard of the conversation, he knew it was probably Reggie Fetherston who had come in to investigate, and had it been a case of a single-handed struggle between them, Tinker would have been perfectly prepared to take his chances.

Fetherston was older than he and of bigger build all round, but Tinker had been up against him before and he figured he would be able to take care of himself —that is, if there were no knife or gun-play. But he knew that, on this occasion, Archie Pherison was waiting on the qui vive outside, and Pherison —well, the dominating one of the trio was a very different proposition.

Then, too, he knew, if what he had overheard was true, Algy Somerton was on the watch at the point of the island only a hundred yards or so away. It looked as if he had got himself into a nasty trap, and he knew it was going to take all his nerve and ingenuity to get out of it. Still he did not move. He could hear the slightly laboured breathing of the gunman as he drew nearer and nearer. Once he encountered some obstruction —probably a protruding nail, Tinker thought —and a soft curse broke the silence. Then Tinker judged that he must be within a yard or so, and his whole body grew suddenly tense as he prepared for action.

It seemed then that Fetherston paused, trying to peer ahead, into the darkness. Tinker knew that it was impossible for him to see anything at the back of the shed from where he stood, but if he took a single stride forward and swept his foot round, he would be sure to encounter his crouching body. Once the Musketeer did that the fireworks would start. But Fetherston did not do so.

Instead, he stood perfectly still for a few moments, then his voice sounded, cold as dripping water.

"If you are in here, come out!" he said in French. "We are too many for you, and you can't get away."

Tinker remained silent. Fetherston also was silent again, but then a faint sound caught Tinker's ears, and he knew the other was beginning to feel his way forward again. Tinker counted slowly up to five, then suddenly he came into action.

As he shot up, like a released spring, he gave vent to a blood-curdling whoop, and the next instant he had driven forward with every ounce of force straight into what he figured would be the Musketeer's body. His guess was better, almost, than he had dared to hope.

His head caught Fetherston just above the stomach, and drove him back against the wall of the shed with a grunt and a crash. Tinker jabbed in a short, vicious left and a hard right to the heart, then he turned and shot out of the shed like an arrow. But if he thought he was to get clean away he was mistaken.

From the moment his companion had entered the shed, Archie Pherison had been on the qui vive, and at the sound of Tinker's yell he knew that Reggie had flushed his bird all right. He had started running towards the opening of the shed, and, just as Tinker shot out like a rabbit, he reached it.

The two crashed together with terrific force, and, although Tinker was moving with greater speed, he did not succeed in sending Pherison down. He did stagger him, and without waiting to pursue his slight advantage, he swung to the right and tried to break clear. Pherison, however, was as quick as lightning. He recovered himself in a flash, and his long arms encircled Tinker's shoulders even as the lad made his break.

Tinker relaxed and dropped quickly, and Archie Pherison gave a curse as his arms slipped down over Tinker's greased body without getting a grip. Tinker bent backwards as far as he could and brought his knee up just as Pherison threw himself upon him.

The shock brought a grunt of pain from the crook, and he rolled to one side. Tinker twisted in the opposite direction and rolled clear just as Reggie Fetherston came staggering out of the shed. Archie Pherison also came to his feet then, and, pausing only long enough to give vent to a loud, shrill whistle—which Tinker rightly guessed was a signal to Algy Somerton —he joined Fetherson in pursuit of the lad.

To make back for the point of the island where he had landed was out of the question for Tinker. The outer bank of the island was still impossible for the same reason as before. It would only take him to the wide stretch of the main river, where the current was too swift and any hope of landing too remote.

His only chance lay in making the near side of the island, where the narrow channel between it and the smaller one which was now between him and the bank, where his hotel stood. And he took that one chance.

Heedless of the bushes which tore at his body, he forced his way through in the direction he hoped would bring him to the edge of the water. He came upon it almost before he was aware he had done so, for the high trees on the other island threw their shadow right across the channel.

He heard a call off to his left, and knew it must be Algy Somerton running down to see what was up. There was no question about the progress of the other two, for he could hear them cursing deeply as they plunged through the bushes after him.

He did not pause to test the depth of the water, but dived in the second his toes reached the edge of the bank, and then, as he came up a few feet out, in the very centre of the current, he turned to the right and began swimming with a powerful crawl stroke.

Somehow, he knew just when the other three, one after the other, took the water. It was plain that they had no intention of abandoning the pursuit, but Tinker knew now that if he could get round the lower point of the smaller island and across to the other bank, he stood a chance of shaking them off.

No amount of determination would drive them on to a pursuit up through the town in their present lack of garments, and, of course, there was always the hope that he would find some late pedestrian, or even a policeman. But the thing was to reach the other bank.

He rounded the point of the smaller island and found himself at once in a tangle of weeds. The long lily-like tentacles wound round his ankles and legs like those of an octopus, and the grease on his limbs did not help him then.

He splashed round frantically trying to break free, and now this new danger threatened to "do" for him quicker than the other. He recalled that, as he had sat in the veranda cafe, he had noticed that same field of weeds, and remembered that it wasn't very large. He could not see just how far it extended towards the island and along that bank, but by the light of the moon he could see clear water on his right, where the current was strong enough to keep the channel clear.

He fought to make that, and, as he twisted round, he saw that his predicament had been seen by his pursuers, who were all three swimming along in the clear water, now quite certain of catching him.

He struggled and fought and tore at the terrible weeds until, by sheer strength, he was clear. He came into clear water at the same moment when one of the Three Musketeers made a wild grab at him.

Once again the grease on his body saved him, and he managed to drive his heel into the face of the one who had attacked him. The same action gave him an impetus, and he began swimming for the near bank with a desperation he had never used before.

As he approached it he saw the bulk of the floating, covered wash-houses —which have already been mentioned —just ahead, and could see that the riverside of the upper one was open to the night. If he could but reach that. He redoubled his efforts, and his pursuers, now seeing his purpose, did the same.

All four swimmers crossed that strip of water as it certainly had never been crossed before, but Tinker's fingers were on the edge of the float first, and he was half-way up before the first of his pursuers —which happened to be Algy Somerton —readied the side.

He caught at Tinker's legs, but again the lad's heel drove backward, sending the Musketeer into the water, and, before one of the others could catch hold, he was on his knees and stumbling forward into the wash-house.

The land side of the float was closed, and Tinker knew, if he were to make the bank, he must first dispose of his pursuers.

He sought about for something to use as a weapon, and came upon a heavy sort of wooden paddle, which he thought must be used for beating the wet clothes, which indeed was the case. He swung round with this in his hand, and sprang back to the edge.

Reggie Fetherston was just climbing up, and without the slightest hesitation, Tinker brought the flat of the wooden paddle down on his head. Fetherston didn't make a sound. He slid back into the water as smoothly as an eel, and as he went under Archie Pherison, who was nearest him, caught at his shoulders. Algy Somerton, on the other hand, repeated his attempt to climb up over the side, but Tinker was ready for him and again brought the paddle down.

Somerton dodged as it descended, but while it missed his head in caught him hard on the shoulder, and he was forced to let go.

Just then Pherison said something, and, instead of trying once more to reach Tinker, Somerton swam along to give him a hand with Fetherston, who was apparently unconscious.

At the same moment a hail came from the bank on the other side of the wash-house. It was in a deep voice in the Normandy patois, and at the sound Archie Pherison and Algy Somerton took Fetherston under the shoulders and began swimming back towards the island.

On his part, Tinker ran along the outer edge of the float —it was about a foot wide —until he came to the lower end of it. There he paused for a moment, but as he saw a figure just coming in sight on the tow-path he dived in and began swimming down stream, hoping to find a place a few hundred yards down where he could land.

He had little fear now of further pursuit on the part of the Three Musketeers, but he had strong reasons for this new move. One was that he had no desire to be seen as he was by any curious native, and the other and stronger was to try, if possible, to reach his quarters without being seen by the Three Musketeers.

What he did not know was that, as he had poised for a moment on the edge of the float, he had been in the full light of the moon, and had been distinctly seen by the man who had appeared on the bank at such an opportune moment.

He swam along quietly past the other two wash-house floats, and then past a float where, in the daytime, one could hire a canoe or skiff. This place, like the others, was in darkness and silence at that hour, and Tinker figured it would be a good place to land. He crawled up on the float, and then crossed cautiously to the bank.

As he did so he thought he saw, some distance upstream, a figure on the bank. Thinking it might be the same man who had seemed curious over the disturbance at the wash-house float, he determined to take cover until the other had gone past. The whole of the shallow bank was covered with long grass, and in this Tinker had no difficulty in concealing himself. He crawled along some little distance and then lay absolutely still, waiting for the other to pass.

He could hear the crunch of boot heels as the late pedestrian came along, and then the smell of strong French tobacco reached his nostrils. The sounds grew plainer and plainer, until they seemed almost opposite him; then suddenly they ceased.

He heard a rustling of grass after a few moments, and, thinking the other had seen him dive into the grass and was intending to dig him out, he drew himself up ready for flight. But the rustling sound stopped then, and he remained motionless until his heart gave a leap as, it seemed scarcely two yards away from him, a low-pitched voice said:

"Try and creep closer to where I am sitting, and tell me just what all this is about."

And as Tinker recognised Sexton Blake's voice he started to obey.

JUST over the bank and across the strand was a railway bridge which crossed the Rue Meissonier, and at that moment a night goods train from the direction of Acheres and Maisons-Lafiitte came through. Under cover of the roar and rattle Tinker covered the short distance that lay between him and Blake, and by the time the rumble had died away, he was lying on one side just behind Blake's broad back.

Then without any preliminary he began and gave Blake a detailed relation of all that had happened since his arrival in Poissy some hours before. Blake listened in silence. He did not make a single comment until the lad had reached the part where he had driven off his pursuers at the bath-house float, and there broke off. Then he sat gazing in the direction of the island towards which two of the Musketeers had assisted their unconscious companion.

It was impossible for him to see, at that distance, whether they had landed on the larger island or had kept on to the one abutting on to the bridge pier. But he had evidently decided not to make an attempt to follow them further that night, for after a little while he said:

"I saw the start of the trouble while I was on the bridge, my lad. I had just come from the inn on the island, and didn't know what was up. I thought then that it must be just some local youths larking about."

"Good heavens, was that you I saw on the bridge, guv'nor?"

"It must have been. There was no one else about as far as I know. But let me go on. As I say, I had been at the inn on the island, and I saw something there, quite as startling in its way, as your experience to-night. I recognised the black man who runs the place. At the Sûreté the prefect stated that the man who ran the inn was, he thought, a Moroccan or Algerian. This he gathered from Coignet's report. But the fellow is neither. Nor is he even a Berber. I recognised him as none other than one of the two Nubians who have served the Three Musketeers in the past. You will remember that one of them was a deaf mute."

"Yes, I remember, guv'nor."

"It was when I saw this Nubian that I began to get a definite suspicion of the identity of the three bandits who have been committing these outrages in and about Paris. And, of course, your experience confirms that. There is not the slightest doubt in my mind now that we are fairly on the track of the men the Sûreté is seeking, and we know that the killings and robberies which have been committed are exactly the type of thing the Three Musketeers are capable of.

"Further than that, we have picked up the trail at the point where poor Coignet dropped it when he was killed and —the Three Musketeers certainly killed Coignet. I think you are correct in feeling that they did not recognise you to-night. If they had got hold of you they should have done so before they finished with you, and it is pretty safe betting that you would have suffered the same fate as the man from the Sûreté. I did not know until I saw you poised on the end of the wash-house float that it was you, but then I could see your black skin in the moonlight and, of course, I drew obvious deductions. You have done remarkably well to-night, my lad —extremely well. But, in my opinion, the usefulness of your present disguise is finished.

"They will endeavour to discover who it was who escaped them to-night. It will be very easy to find out that a person of your description is staying at the Esturgeon. And from that to the discovery of your real identity is only a short step. We shall have to think up some means of baffling them without getting out of our stride, for I have a feeling that time is precious and that if we are to lay our hands on them we shall have to do so very soon. We must not forget the conversation you overheard on that island over there. So just lie quiet until I think a bit. By the way, are you cold?"

"Not a bit, guv'nor."

Nevertheless, Blake slipped off his outer coat and passed it back to the lad who pulled it over his shoulders and sat hunched up waiting while his master attacked the problem which had arisen as a result of their joint adventures that evening.

For perhaps a quarter of an hour or so he smoked in silence, then as another train rattled across the bridge and dashed along in the direction of Villennes, he leant back and said:

"I think I have hit on the first step we must take, Tinker. Now listen carefully. Can you get back into your room at the Esturgeon without being forced to rouse someone?"

"Yes, guv'nor. I can get up over the veranda and right into my room by the big chestnut at the corner of the building —the same one by which I reached the water."

"Good. I take it you have with you the mixture for removing that black stain?"

"Yes, sir."

"Then listen. I have an idea. We must try to impress the three principals as well as the Nubian, Abdul, that the affair tonight was of no real importance. That impression must be given without delay, but to do so I shall have to get on the telephone to Paris, and I think the best course will be to reveal my identity to the local commissaire of police and use the police wire.

"In the meantime, you get into your room and prepare to leave as early as possible in the morning. You will be able to get a train soon after five o'clock in the direction of Paris. Take it, get out at Acheres, which is right on the edge of the forest of St. Germain and make your way to a secluded part of the forest. There you can find an opportunity to remove the black stain and change your disguise. You can put on something to answer until you rejoin me.

"Come back to Poissy as soon as you can and make straight for the Rendezvous des Pecheurs, where I am staying. Before you can get there I shall leave word that I expect a young friend. In my room you will find anything further you may need to add to your disguise. You may find me there or you may not. In any event, stay under cover in my room until I come in. By that time I hope I shall have succeeded in convincing the black on the island that what happened to-night had no real importance, and we shall have to figure that he will lose no time in communicating this to the Three Musketeers.

"I don't know what they are up to now, but we shall have to take the risk that they will still be in this neighbourhood. Now follow me at a distance. Keep under cover of the trees as much as you can, and I will give you a hand up on to the verandah roof at the Esturgeon."

With that Blake rose, and putting on his coat walked leisurely along the towpath until he came to a set of stone steps leading up the bank to the strand. He mounted those and, turning to the left, set off along the deserted strand in the direction of the Esturgeon, which stood at the far end directly facing him.

As has already been said, the Strand had at some time in the past been planted with three closely set rows of trees which, when in leaf, gave a gracious shade by day and made the place almost gloomy at night. Taking advantage of these trees, Tinker did not find it difficult to dodge along not very far behind Blake, and so carefully did he work that not unless someone in one of the windows of one of the houses actually facing on the Strand had been on the watch could he have been spotted. And it was unlikely that anyone in a house there would be at a window at that hour of the night.

Reaching the last row of trees near the hotel, Blake paused and waited. While he stood in the shadow a slim dark figure slipped past him and just flashed for a second in the moonlight before sinking into the shadow cast by the enormous chestnut at the corner of the building.

Blake then walked across until he, too, was in the same shadow bulk, and found Tinker standing with his hands gripped round an upright ready to go up.

Blake gave him a hand and a powerful hoist which sent the lad up clean on to the roof of the verandah; then as he disappeared from view Blake strolled across to his own hotel and inserted in the lock the key which had been given him by the proprietaire.

But Blake only spent a few minutes in his room. He sat there in the dark until Tinker signalled across from his own window that he had arrived in his room safely. Then Blake rose, and once more left the inn.

This time he took a course away from the river, following the main street along under the railway bridge there until he came to the bureau of the commissaire of police. There was a single "agent" on duty in the rather dingy little office which was in reality at one end of the very ancient mairie and town hall.

It took Blake a considerable time to impress the agent on duty that his business was sufficiently urgent and private for the commissaire to be disturbed at that hour of the night, for it was now past one o'clock.

There was nothing impressive about the shabbily-dressed fisherman who made the demand, and at first the agent appeared to think his visitor had had too much to drink.

But when Blake took out a certain pink card which had been given him at the Prefecture in Paris the other came to life in a flash. He got on the telephone (a private line) to the commissaire's house, and, after a few moments' conversation, that gentleman said he would see the visitor if he would come along to the house. This Blake readily agreed to do, and after receiving detailed instructions from the agent how to reach it, he started off.

It appeared that the commissaire lived along the road which runs from the back of the town hall at Poissy to Maisons-Laffitte, and in about five minutes he reached it.

He found a sleepy stout man waiting for him, and at first the commissaire seemed inclined, like the agent, to look upon his late visitor as a practical joker. But the sight of the pink card and another document which disclosed Blake's real identity, soon altered his manner, and he at once consented to try and get through to the Prefect in Paris along the police line.

It was only after considerable delay that he succeeded in doing so, but eventually he was put through to Monsieur Dupuis' private apartments at the Sûreté, and when he heard the first few sentences of Blake's conversation with the Prefect his last doubts vanished.

While the detective talked he listened and studied him, and gradually he saw, beneath the disguise, the real man of whom he had heard so much in police and criminal investigation circles. But he was no end puzzled at the request Blake had to make of the Prefect; nor, when he had finished, did Blake enlighten him. He merely said:

"I am greatly obliged to you, M. le Commissaire. M. Dupuis has consented to do as I have asked him. And now I wish to know if it will be possible for you to have two men detailed at an early hour in the morning on the bridge. Soon after six o'clock the man I have asked the Prefect to send should arrive from Paris. He will go direct from the train to the inn on the island which abuts on to the bridge, and soon after his arrival there I think there will be a disturbance. In this case, I want the two men you detail for the job to rush into the inn and interfere. Following that, I want them to make a pretence of arresting the man who starts the trouble. They will have no difficulty in picking the right man, for he will be a black man—like the proprietaire of the inn. Will you arrange this?"

"Of a surety, M. Blake. But what shall we do with him after?"

"Let him slip away quietly and return to Paris. His work here will be finished. And I have only to add, M. le Commissaire, that my work here has to do with the death of M. Coignet, of the Sûreté, and is necessarily of the most secret nature."

The commissaire puffed with importance.

"Fear not, monsieur," he said, "nothing shall leak out."

Blake thanked him and took his departure. As he gained the road and started back towards the main street, he muttered:

"If the prefect's man keeps to schedule and understands his job, it ought to work. But it will have to be brought off early. And Tinker must absolutely disappear from the scene. I shall have to be about early to see how things go."

With that he struck into a long stride which soon brought him to the main street, where he turned, passed down under the railway bridge, and then turned the corner near the bridge, which brought him to his own small inn. He saw not a soul on the way, nor, after reaching his room, did he see any signs of the Three Musketeers, or even Tinker.

He undressed and slipped into bed, but before he dozed off he marked the hour of five o'clock in his mind, and such an old campaigner was he, that it was on the exact minute of the time he had set himself that he woke.

Blake dressed and slipped out of the Rendezvous des Pecheurs before anyone else was astir. Before descending he glanced across towards the corner window of the Esturgeon, but although the window was open, he could not tell whether Tinker was still there or not.

As a matter of fact, Tinker had taken his departure not ten minutes before, and was even then standing on the railway station, waiting for an early train for Paris, from which he intended dropping off at Acheres.

On emerging from the inn, Blake, carrying a long-handled fishing-net, creel, and a three-jointed bamboo rod, walked leisurely towards the bridge, and, turning there, strolled across in the direction of the fourth pier against which the island abutted.

There were already several persons of the workman class to be seen, for down in Normandy most of the folk are astir early, and, as is the custom, the greater number of them stop at one of the numerous cafes for morning coffee, with a dash of rum in it.

Blake was counting on finding the inn on the island already open for this sort of custom, and, as he walked along, he found his guess was a good one, for he saw several small groups of workmen coming across the bridge from the Italian colony on the other side of the river.

It was a cool morning, with the mist still lying low on the water, but with the sky above giving promise of a warm day.

On the far side of the river where the current runs deepest a tug was already at work, drawing a string of heavily-laden barges towards the locks, three-quarters of a mile above, and downstream other barges could be seen taking their rate of progress from the current alone.

A few fishing enthusiasts were already to be seen in punts tied among the myriad stakes just above the bridge, and, as he was in no particular hurry, Blake leant over the side, smoking and watching them. He spent about a quarter of an hour in this fashion, taking note at the same time of those who went in and left the inn on the island.

Then, as he glanced to his right towards the town, whence had come the sound of a train, he saw an engine just crossing the main street by the railway bridge, and, by the string of passenger coaches behind, he knew that the early train had just arrived from Paris.

At the same moment another train came rumbling along from Villennes, and as it slowed down for Poissy, he thought that this one ought to be the one which Tinker would take. Which, indeed, was the case. He thought, too, that if the prefect in Paris had succeeded in doing as he had requested, the man he expected should have arrived by the other train.

It did not take him long to discover that M. Dupuis had not failed him, for as he still gazed townwards, he saw a heavily-built black man swing into view, and almost at the same instant a couple of gendarmes appeared at the same end of the bridge.

Blake knocked the dottle from his pipe, and continued his way towards the iron gate at the head of the steps which led down to the inn on the island.

He descended and crossed the front garden to the open door, through which he could see several workmen gathered about the bar. He entered and made his way to the far end, noting as he did so that the big Nubian, Abdul, was behind the bar, and was being assisted by a heavily-built slattern of a woman, whose features were more those of the Mediterranean water-front than of Normandy. He thought to himself that Abdul must have brought the woman from either Marseilles or Alexandria, and he was right.

He set his fishing gear in one corner, and called for a coffee and rum. The woman served him, and, he had just drawn it towards him when there was a commotion at the door, and into the place came lurching the same husky-looking black he had seen cross the road from the railway station.

One glance at the man, and Blake knew that the prefect had been able to lay his hands on the man he wanted, for the newcomer was a pure Senegalese, and it was of such a man the prefect had spoken.

As a matter of fact, the Senegalese who had just appeared, had, at no distant date, been notorious in certain boxing circles in France, and had it not been for his record in the French Colonial troops during the war, he would have seen the inside of a prison long before.

But, instead of permitting him to pursue such a course, the shrewd prefect of police in Paris had laid his hands on him and had impressed him into police service. In that work he had proved himself just as valuable to M. Dupuis as before he had been a nuisance, for there are many thousands of French Colonial coloured subjects in Paris, and, so complicated are the numerous questions that are continually arising concerning them, that a separate police department has had to be formed to deal with them.

It was in this work that the ex-pugilist, drunkard and trouble maker, had proved so valuable; and, strange to say, he had taken to police work like a duck to water. In case of trouble among those of his own colour, he was the first to be sent to settle it; and, what with the police authority he now enjoyed, and his previous reputation as a ring champion and "tough," he usually managed to quell the turbulent ones without much difficulty.

And it was when M. Dupuis heard that Sexton Blake wanted a black man whom he could trust, to come to Poissy for a certain purpose, that the prefect had at once thought of his new recruit.

As the Senegalese lurched into the place, those at that end of the bar drew back a little. The man looked in a raging temper over something, and, from his manner, it appeared as if he had already had enough to drink, despite the early hour.

His eye was savage and roaming. His thick lips were parted, and seemed to be flecked with foam. His long arms swung back and forth like those of an impatient gorilla, and his head was hunched forward as if challenging the world. A white man couldn't have done it so well. Only a being not very far removed from the savage life of the jungle could have evinced that form of rage.

"Get mad —get angry —act angry!" the prefect had said, and all the way down from Paris the Senegalese had been working himself up, until now he was almost as genuinely raging as he appeared. That

68

was the jungle nature responding to the savage urge.

He hit heavily against the bar and glared at the other black man who faced him. The Nubian was a bigger man but soft, and without the savage courage of the other. Abdul would not hesitate to tackle any six of the sort of clients who came to the inn on the island, but a Senegalese was a very different proposition, and the flabby Nubian knew it.

Further, he must have been inwardly amazed to see such a client in a place such as Poissy. Blake knew that the Nubian was in a dead funk, despite the fact that he showed his white teeth in a wide smile.

"Bon jour, my friend," he said in French. "You are a newcomer here. It is good to see one of one's own colour. What can I serve you?"

The Senegalese brought his thick right arm round and sent the Italians near him staggering away. There was a little muttering at this, but one look and a savage curse silenced them.

Then the Senegalese continued to glare at the Nubian. For almost a full minute he stood thus, then, slowly and deliberately, he spat straight into the face of Abdul. The Nubian stepped back, and his eyes flashed with rage. His hand rose as if he would hurl the glass he had been wiping into the face of the Senegalese, but those raging, jungle eyes still flashed, and he wilted.

"Rum, strong double rum!" snarled the Senegalese, and meekly the Nubian turned to obey.

The glass was emptied at a single gulp, then the Senegalese turned, and slowly his eyes swept the crowd. Every Italian and native in the place flinched under the glare with the exception of the fisherman who stood at the other end of the bar. The Senegalese seemed to take more note of him than the others, for he knew that one among that crowd must be the man the prefect had told him needed him in Poissy. But he was not sure, so he turned back to Abdul and began to speak, or rather to talk and curse at the same time.

He began with an appalling insult, and then he flayed the Nubian back and forth and up and down until the soft black went green under the insults. And those who were there gradually gathered what it was that had put the Senegalese in such a rage.

He was angry, and he was going to have satisfaction, it seemed. The night before he had come to Poissy, and had gone in from the bank under the first arch of the bridge for a swim. While he was swimming about three men had come from this very inn on this very island and had set upon him.

He had not wished trouble, and they were three to one. He had tried to escape by swimming down-stream, but they had driven him to another island. He had had a fight with them there, but had again escaped and had been forced to swim again.

He had succeeded in making one of the floats which one could see from the bridge, and there he had driven them off. But he had not come to this place to be hounded and attacked. He, too, could fight, and would fight.

And he wanted to know who those three men were. He had waited all night until the inn should open in the morning. He, the thug behind the bar, knew who those three would be. Their names, and quickly. Where could he find them? Were they even now in the bar? Speak, and quickly.

That was the sum and substance of what one could gather from the terrible curse-laden harangue, and, watching closely, Sexton Blake saw a queer expression flash into the eyes of the Nubian. He was in fear, in deadly fear of this raging savage in front of him; but, even in the midst of that fear, Blake could have named the fleeting expression as one of relief more than anything else.

He stammered and stuttered, and denied that anyone could have been attacked by persons from his inn. As he made the denial the Senegalese gave utterance to just three words, villainous, vicious words they were; then he seemed to turn into a human cyclone.

With one terrific heave he brought the whole bar over with a crash. In another move he had caught up a heavy wooden chair, and, before the Nubian could save himself, the Senegalese was upon him, shrieking and cursing, and promising him much worse if his swimming was again interfered with.

He beat Abdul down to his knees, and then to his face. He struck again and again and spared not, and, even while the big Nubian was a heaving mass of beaten black blubber, sobbing and cursing and denying in one breath, the Senegalese turned and made for the dozen or so workmen who still remained.

There was a general stampede for the door, but before they could get through the Senegalese had brought the chair down crashing a dozen times, and, as they managed to squeeze through into the garden, they took to their heels.

70

It was just then that the two gendarmes who had been strolling across the bridge came running down the steps, and, despite the threatening attitude of the Senegalese, they rushed him.

There was a brief struggle, but as one of the gendarmes jerked out his automatic and jammed the muzzle against the forehead of the apparently crazed negro, he gave in and relaxed, panting and glaring at the Nubian, who was attempting to get to his feet.

The rather shabbily clad fisherman had kept his position all this time except when the bar had come crashing over, when he had been forced to step back a little. But now, as the two gendarmes secured their prisoner, he picked up his fishing-gear and made for the door. They did not attempt to stop him, and as he reached the bridge he saw the battered remnants of the clients making good speed for the opposite shore.

Blake walked along and took the tow-path which would bring him to the boat float above the bridge, where he could engage a punt for fishing. But he paused under the outjutting wing of a very old building, and gazed back.

As he watched he saw the two gendarmes appear with the Senegalese between them, and as they dragged their prisoner across the bridge, the shabbily clad fisherman thoughtfully filled his pipe. He waited until they had disappeared from view, then, as he touched a match to the shag, he moved on again towards the float.

But those who had been in the inn during the sensational morning upheaval would have been considerably intrigued had they heard the fisherman mutter to himself in English:

"It was a genius stroke. The prefect could not have picked a better man for the job. It almost deceived me, who knew what to expect. I am willing to wager that Abdul is fully convinced now of the identity of the swimmer last night, and, that being so, he will lose no time in communicating with the Three Musketeers. That is bound to be his move, wherever they are. And that is the next riddle to be solved. I must locate them inside the next forty-eight hours, or they will still stand a good chance of getting clear. I'll keep an eye on that island during the morning, and if Abdul goes off anywhere Tinker may be here to follow him. At any rate, I can do nothing until the lad arrives."

With that Blake hailed the owner of the float, and began to dicker for the hire of a fishing punt; but he was wrong in thinking that

Abdul's move would be the next one. The Three Musketeers themselves were to leave a blood mark before many hours had passed.

POISSY, on the River Seine, ranks among the oldest and most historical towns in all France. When Paris was the Lutetia of the Romans, and London was the Londinium of Caesar's legions, there was already a small hamlet where Poissy now stands, for just at that point there was shallow water which made one of the few fords in some miles.

Later on, when the Vikings swept across the North Sea, and, after harrying Britain, carried their adventures and the aggressive prows of their many-oared galleys across the Channel to Gaul and up the Seine, even to the gates of Paris, Poissy was a stopping point en route.

It was a little later when the Normans conquered the King of Paris —for in those days the King of Paris was not necessarily the King of France any more than he was King of Brittany or King of Navarre —and then, as the centuries passed, and all ancient Gaul became consolidated under the single banner of a King of France, it became a point of strategy, its ford was spanned by a bridge — remnants of which are still incorporated in the later structure of the Twelfth Century —and the Holy Church of Rome found it an attractive and fruitful spot for the purposes of Mother Church.

For a hundred kilometers and more from Poissy down the Seine to Rouen, the valley is green and smiling and fertile, kept rich and deeply silted from the regular overflowing of the river, just in the same way that the valley of the Nile in Egypt is enriched by the torrents that sweep down from Abyssinia. And at no point is the soil richer than at Poissy.

The old church —now ranked as a cathedral —is a pure and graceful structure of Gothic design, and, although it has in many parts fallen into disrepair, it has not yet been spoilt by the vandal hands of the modern restorer.

But even before Rome planted the foundations of this ancient church it had already begun the erection of an abbey, and to-day the great entrance, with its twin towers and heavy, beamed arches, still stands just as it was first built, stone by stone and course by course centuries ago. At that time Mother Church was all powerful in France. Rome ruled all Europe, even England, and the Church selected and held the richest plums throughout the domains where it ruled.

It was the same at Poissy. For a good half-mile, straight back from the bank of the Seine, was the domain of the abbey, and in width it was anything from a quarter to half a mile.

Almost adjoining that again was the domain of the church proper; and, combined, they composed the major portion of what is Poissy of to-day. There the monks lived a cloistered life, while the lay brothers toiled in the fields or carried on the eternal round of building until the Abbey of Poissy was one of the richest in the north of France, and the sharp-pointed, Gothic spire of the church was the landmark of the rule of Rome in all that part.

From time to time bits of the old abbey demesne were lopped off here and there, and to-day much of it is occupied by the houses of the citizens of modern republican France. But, as has been said, the core, so to speak, of the old abbey still remains, and no vandal hand has yet touched the rich, virgin park which was laid down by the monks of old.

One can stroll through the ancient outer gate and pass immediately into an old-world cloister of peace and beauty which is almost overwhelming in its suddenness. Just above the main gate is the old gate-house, still occupied, and, from the inside, a beautiful bank of thick, green ivy.

Along the old cobbled, winding path one can find the inner gate, glimpsing from time to time gardens of northern green but tropic density and colour. There are the old buildings of the monks —the grain houses and stables, the abbot's house and the convocation house.

The sheds and wine cellars and a host of other thick-walled barns and cells, with only slits in the stone to permit the passage of air and light. It is to step into the atmosphere of pre-mediaeval France, and the distant hoot of a motor-horn sounds gratingly on the ear and strangely incongruous in those old-world surroundings.

The church was the christening spot of the good King Louis, who was afterwards canonised and is now known as St. Louis. The church is more identified with him than with any other monarch, for Queen Blanche, mother of St. Louis, loved Poissy, and would visit there whenever opportunity occurred.

It was this same Queen Blanche who built the old mill, remains of which are still to be seen at the end of the ancient bridge, and it was she who founded the convent, parts of which can still be seen in a tangled old park which lies between the cathedral and the river.

These few historical facts may seem to have little bearing on the present story, but if it had not been for the old abbey there, and the later founding of the convent and the building of the mill by Queen Blanche, this story had never been written, or, rather, the Three Musketeers would have been compelled to seek their lair elsewhere, as will presently be seen.

So it must be borne in mind that on one hand the old abbey domain stretched in a long, heavily-wooded slope for a half-mile to the river, that close at hand the church lay with its grounds reaching down to the convent; and that, from here, the church demesne stretched again to the river, parallel with that of the abbey, and with one corner touching the end of the bridge where the mill of Queen Blanche had been built.

Now, shortly after seven o'clock on the same morning that Sexton Blake was present at the disturbance in the inn on the island by the bridge, and his assistant had taken the train for Acheres to seek a secluded spot in the forest of St. Germain where he might effect a change in his disguise, three persons in the garb of brothers of the order of Benedictine monks sat talking in a small, cell-like chamber which was situated underground in one of the oldest portions of an inner part of the old abbey buildings, and which was lighted only by a narrow slit in the stone wall high up, close to the roof.

It was of the type of cell used as a penance chamber by the monks, and its furnishings were as meagre as they had ever been in the days when it was in active employ.

There were three narrow iron cots, each having a thin straw mattress and pillow. Two blankets went to each cot, and in one corner was a small, tripod, iron wash-stand, with, on the floor beside it, an enamel jug of cold water. The floor was of stone slabs, worn in hollows but swept clean.

There was a small deal table in the centre of the room, on which reposed three enamelware plates, three metal forks, knives and spoons. Three tin mugs and a cheap pressed-glass dish of salt completed the table accoutrements.

There was a long "yard" of bread, some bits of cold meat, and the remains of a head of lettuce —what was left of the frugal morning repast which the three in monk's garb had partaken of.

In the stone wall opposite that in which the arrow slit of a

75

window had been built was a door, partly ajar, but the chamber beyond was dark, and it was impossible to see more than a few inches beyond the threshold. Each of the three sat on a cot, and two of them were giving attention to what the third was saying.

He was speaking in such a low tone that, even if one had crouched close to the window-slit above, one would not have been able to hear what he was saying. But it was evident from their demeanour that the conversation was of considerable import.

"We've got to wind things up sharp now," were his words. "That business last night —might have been nothing or it might have been a lot. It is mighty queer why that nigger happened to be just there when we broke the surface. We muddled things badly on that island. It was my fault in a way. When Reggie said he was going to search the shed, I didn't think the fellow could be there. But he was, and he got away. It seemed to me that his whole body was greased. I had a good hold of him, but my arms slipped off as if I had been trying to hold a greased pig."

"And that is just what it was, Archie," put in one of the others. "I had a grab at him at the pier when we first spotted him and felt the same thing. Did you notice it, Reggie?"

"I did, Algy, my boy," drawled the third. "But don't ask me anything just now. My head is still splitting where he caught me with that club at the wash-house float. And if you two hadn't been forced to look after me you would have caught him. Then it wouldn't have taken long to find out what he was about. It's queer, though, how anxious he was not to be caught."

The first speaker, who was Archie Pherison, shrugged. "He may have just been a scared coon," he said. "We went after him pretty savagely, and he may have heard what happened to the other man a few nights ago. Just the same, I'd like to be sure. We can take it that Dupuis isn't going to give up now. But I haven't been able to spot anyone else that looks like one of his men. Anyway, I think we'd better wind up our ball of yarn down here and make a getaway while the going is good. By the time we reach Havre the Sultan ought to be about due, and if she isn't there we can lie low until she turns up. If we get away to-night we can dump the stuff with Wertheim in Paris and let him settle up with us later. We can pack the actual money along with us —Cardolak will see that it is changed for us all right without leaving any trail. Besides, even without the jewels and pieces, we have a nice haul of cash to take along. It would be unwise to overplay our hand."

"I agree with that," put in Algy Somerton. "Still, you said Archie, we might pull off just one more stunt before we light out."

"I have that in mind all right, but there is only one thing I can see that we can tackle."

"You mean?"

"I mean —Ssh! What was that?"

As he spoke Archie Pherison reached beneath the skirt of his monk's dress and jerked out a heavy automatic pistol. The other two followed suit swiftly, and all three swung towards the partially open door that led to the inner chamber. Strange weapons and strange actions for three Benedictine monks.

They sat listening tensely; then sharply Pherison called:

"Who is there?"

There came a faint sound as if stone was clanging upon stone, and then a deep voice, husky in the effort to smother it.

"It is I, masters," was the reply. And at once all three weapons were lowered, while Archie Pherison said:

"Is it you, Abdul? Come in, then. What brings you here?"

The door swung back then, and Abdul of the inn on the island, his face bruised and swollen from the beating he had received, came into the cell. The Three Musketeers gazed in amazement at the picture he presented, and Archie Pherison's voice was sharp as he asked:

"What has happened? Speak up, man!"

The big Nubian salaamed and stood just within the door. Then he said:

"It is about what happened last night, masters. I have had proof this morning that it was all but chance."

"What do you mean, Abdul? Explain yourself," ordered Pherison impatiently.

"It is this, masters. As usual, I opened the inn for the early morning trade, which, as you know, comes mostly from the Italian labour colony over the river. While I was attending to the clients, a black man, a stranger, a Senegalese or Nigerian, I think, came into the place in a state of great anger. He ordered a coffee and rum, and drank it off at once. Then he began to upbraid me in very violent terms. He was a very bad specimen, masters, and before I could remonstrate with him he began speaking of what had occurred last night. He said that he was a stranger here, and had gone for a bathe in the river. He said that three persons had set upon him, and had tried to do him injury. He said also that the three persons had come from my island, and demanded that they be shown to him. I made some denial, but he did not believe me, and before I could reason with him he had seized hold of the bar and pulled it over by main force. He was very powerful, and, masters, I am no fighter of that sort. He next picked up a chair and began to assault me. I was powerless to defend myself, and he beat me to the floor. Then he set about what clients were still in the place, and drove them forth. I do not know what might have followed, but for the timely arrival of two gendarmes, who took him into custody, and dragged him off. But it was he whom you saw in the river last night, and, from what occurred this morning, it is plain that he had nothing to do with the police or —that other matter. As soon as possible, masters, I made my way here to tell you what had taken place."

"And you did well, Abdul," said Archie Pherison. "I —we are indeed sorry that you have suffered at this fellow's hands, but you shall not be the loser thereby. We shall see to that. And it is important that we should know it was no spy in the river last night. If he had but said something, we should have let him go."

"Isn't it rather queer that he didn't?" put in Algy Somerton. "He did not appear half as aggressive last night as he seems to have been this morning, judging from what Abdul has to tell us."

"He had been drinking heavily this morning, masters," put in the Nubian.

"Last night he was probably scared stiff at the way we popped up out of the water," put in Archie Pherison in English. "You know what a coon is at night and with a moon," he added, and the trio of crooks grinned in unison. Then, in French, Pherison went on:

"Is that all, Abdul?"

"Yes, masters. There have been no other signs. One man who was at the inn last night for a little was there again this morning. He is a stranger, but is just one of the fishermen who come to this place. From an upper window of the inn I saw him in a punt above the bridge before I came here."

"Very well, Abdul. You had better return to the inn now, and keep a sharp lookout all day. We are discussing matters now, and we shall probably be leaving here very soon. There are certain matters to attend to first, and it is just possible that you may see us at the inn during the day. If we should come in haste be ready for us, for we shall need to get under cover quickly. But I do not think you will see us that way. At any rate, we shall communicate with you. Now, you had better get back, and by the way you came. Have a care that you are not seen."

"Never fear, masters; I shall tread with care. The woman is on guard, and she understands my signals." And with that the Nubian salaamed and withdrew.

They sat waiting until they once more heard that odd, clanging sound as of stone against stone; then Archie Pherison returned his automatic to a pocket beneath the monk's robe, an action which the others duplicated, and said:

"Well, fellows, that is one bit of good news. I was a bit leery of that nigger last sight, but what Abdul has told us settles it. He was just some stray nigger that was stiff with fear in the moonlight, but got his courage up with a few hooches this morning, and started out looking for blood. Don't you agree?"

The other two indicated by nods that they did, and Pherison went on:

"That decides us about the other thing as well. We will do as we first intended —bring off one more stunt before we go, and we will bring it off right here in Poissy, too. I fancy that will give our friend the prefect something to think about. And then, while, his men are chasing themselves around here, we shall be well away, and as soon as we have dropped the stuff with Wertheim, in Paris, we will make for Havre and pick up the Sultan. Is that agreed?"

They nodded their agreement; then Reggie Fetherston said:

"Just what is the idea, Archie —the one we have already discussed?"

"Yes, the local bank here. We shall need to use the car, and work it about the same as the last bank stunt. You know, fellows, that here in Poissy the two banks are branches of the big Paris banks, just like most of the banks round about the city, and like the one we tapped before. Well, the two days in the week that the one I have in mind is open are Tuesday and Friday. To-day being Friday, it means that the branch manager comes down from Paris this morning with funds for the day, and, as there was a local market yesterday, it seems that a pretty good lump of stuff ought to be deposited this morning. My idea is to get there just a few minutes before twelve. That is the last hour for several reasons, but principally because most of the deposits will have been made by then, and we ought to get the bulk of those, as well as what was brought down from Paris, for the daily transactions. And, as I said, we shall have to use the car."

"That car will be getting pretty well known by now even if we have changed the colour panels each time," remarked Algy Somerton.

Pherison shrugged.

"We shall have to chance that," he replied. "And it will be the last time. We cannot take it with us. It will be too risky. We shall get rid of it after the hold-up to-day, and then to-night we shall get the stuff together. Now, listen, and I will tell you what I think will be the best plan —at least the one which, in my opinion, will give us most chance of success. When I have finished, if either of you can suggest any improvement, by all means do so."

And with that he began to speak in deliberate, low tones, explaining his plan. The other two crooks listened closely to what he had to say, and did not interrupt until he had finished. Then there was a brief silence, which Algy Somerton broke.

"I suppose I take the wheel," he said.

"Yes, of course."

"It will probably be necessary to shoot," remarked Reggie Fetherston.

"Then we shall have to do so, and, if we do, shoot to kill —as usual," answered Archie Pherison brutally. "We must take no chances on this, our last, stunt. If complications arise, we shall have to make for Abdul's island, but our best chance will be to make for the forest, as I have suggested. But Algy will be in the car, and that will be up to him. Now, let us rest for a little. We shall need it."

CHAPTER 11. *According to Plan —What Happened In the Forest —Three Monks and a Wrecked Car.*

AT precisely a quarter past eleven that morning the three individuals, clad in the monkish vestments of priests of the Benedictine order, and with wide black felt hats on their heads, entered the black, cell-like chamber from which Abdul, the Nubian, had appeared, and wound their way up a narrow, corkscrew iron staircase to the floor above, which was level with the ground.

The room into which they emerged was also of stone —floor and walls and ceiling —and, in days gone by, had been an outer receiving-room of the convocation house.

It should, perhaps, be explained here that this part of the old abbey and another building at the extreme western end of the domain still remains in the hands of the church, although neither of the buildings is very much used. Indeed, until the arrival of the three Benedictine pilgrims, who now lived in the two cell-like rooms of the convocation house, they had been unoccupied for months; but there had been no difficulty about three monks of the well-known order being allowed their use while resting at Poissy before resuming their pilgrimage. That was how the Three Musketeers came to be in that quiet retreat, where it would never have occurred for anyone to seek them, even if the three pilgrim monks had aroused any curiosity.

They took good care that they should be seen abroad very little; certainly there was not the faintest suspicion to connect them with the three criminals whom Coignet of the Sûreté had traced as far as the inn on the island. It is a question if half a dozen persons in Poissy knew that the three pilgrims were occupying the old cells at the convocation house.

From the room on the ground floor an old wooden door gave access to a tangled little garden, which in turn opened on to one of the ancient cobbled lanes that intersected the domain. By this they reached the inner gate house, and, after passing through the arch, traversed another cobbled lane, until they came to the outer gatehouse.

This brought them to the main road outside the high stone wall which still surrounds the abbey domain, and almost opposite the cathedral.

Once in the main road, they turned to the right, and, with slow

81

step and downcast eyes, walked slowly up the hill past the whitewashed walls of the House of Correction, then past the graveyard, and on until they came to a deserted part, where, between white-painted modern gates, they could see the garden and front of a modern villa.

Until a couple of years previously, this villa had been occupied during the summer months by a Paris merchant who had been in the habit of installing his family there from May to October, while he himself would come down for each week-end.

But two years before, while on a visit to France, Mathew Cardolak, the mystery multi-millionaire of Boston, had spent a day in Poissy, and through some notion —perhaps a fleeting fancy, or perhaps with a glimpse into the future when such a retreat might prove useful —he had purchased the place.

At that, it was but one of many which he possessed in many parts of the globe, and it was one of the factors which had influenced the Three Musketeers in their choice of Poissy as headquarters during their recent campaign of crime in and about Paris —that, and what Mathew Cardolak had at one time told Archie Pherison about the old abbey there.

Cardolak himself had not seen the place since he had bought it, and for the last two years it had been in the care of one of his creatures —in this instance a Greek mechanic and his wife. The mechanic was accustomed to act as the millionaire's chauffeur whenever his master came to France. And, of course, there had been no difficulty in the Three Musketeers getting the use of the place while they were there. But they were too shrewd to use it as actual headquarters. The cell beneath the convocation house was far more suitable for a lair, but Cardolak's villa served another purpose, which shall be seen.

Archie Pherison opened one of the white gates and the other two monks followed him through. Then the three, still keeping their devout pose, walked up the gravelled drive and round the corner of the house until they were at the back of the house and invisible from the road.

No glance of recognition passed between him and the three monks, but it seemed that he must be of the church of Rome instead of the orthodox Greek church, for he greeted the three pilgrims with every sign of reverence. Each returned the salutation with a slight gesture, and then, in response to an invitation, they followed the caretaker into the house.

It was a large cosy kitchen into which he led them, and once the door was closed, shutting off the view of any prying eyes from the road, the manner of the three monks underwent a sudden change. It was Archie Pherison who spoke:

"Well, Goulokos," he said in French, "is the car ready?"

"Oui, monsieur," was the reply. "I can have it ready for the road in a few minutes."

"That is well, for we wish to use it. Our clothes —are they in the garage?"

"Oui, monsieur."

"Then we shall come with you. It will be better to go by the passage."

The Greek turned, and, opening a door, ushered them into a covered passage that led along from the kitchen to the stable. From here another door gave access into a small garage where a low-slung powerful-looking roadster was standing. At the moment its colour was dark red, but, as he entered the garage, Algy Somerton (who usually took charge of the wheel of any car used by the Three Musketeers) walked across, and, after fumbling for a few moments beneath the switchboard, turned a button.

Immediately there was a sound as if a slatted Venetian blind had been let fall, and, had one been observing the body of the car, one would have seen that the red had suddenly given place to dark blue.

Again Algy Somerton turned the switch, and once more there was the same sound as of slats tumbling, and this time the body of the car changed to a bright green. And at that he left it.

It was all simple enough. The body had been constructed with several closely-fitted coloured veneer panels; one set superimposed on the other, there being five in all. The cabinet work had been done so finely that it was difficult to see any signs of jointure, and where these necessary lines did exist, the painter had inserted a plain gold stripe which looked perfectly natural as trimming, whichever colour happened to be in use at the moment.

Each set of veneer panels was controlled by an electric device which worked them automatically, much as the ordinary roller blind is worked, and a touch was sufficient to change from one set to another, thus making it possible to effect a very material alteration in the appearance of the car even while running at top speed.

It was this simple device which explained why the "low-slung, powerful roadster" that had been identified on so many occasions with the three bandits who had been committing outrages in and about Paris, had been differently described on each occasion.

When Archie Pherison and Reggie Fetherston nodded their approval at the colour he had chosen for that day, Algy Somerton joined them at the back of the car. An open suitcase was now lying on the floor, from which the other two had chosen some garments, and Algy followed suit.

While the Greek mechanic busied himself over the engine, the three crooks doffed their monkish robes and proceeded to get into ordinary garments. These consisted of dark lounge suits and plain flannel shirts, and when this part of the change was completed they all put on wide-brimmed stetson hats, which they pulled well down over the eyes.

They then slipped into long, neutral-coloured motoring coats, into the right-hand side-pockets of which they dropped automatic pistols.

By this time the mechanic had completed his examination and pronounced everything in order. Archie Pherison looked at the clock in the front of the car.

"Twenty minutes to twelve," he announced. "Just time to start. Get the doors open, Goulokos."

The Greek hesitated.

"What time will you return, monsieur?"

"We shall not return —with the car," answered Archie Pherison coolly. "You may or may not see us again before we leave. I cannot say that; but, in any event, we shall send you money through Mr. Cardolak. As for the car, we shall dispose of that as we have planned, and if you hear rumours of an abandoned car being found, you will be well advised, Goulokos, not to lay claim to it." And as he uttered the words the bandit smiled as if at a joke.

Then the Greek opened the double doors of the garage, Pherison and Fetherston climbed into the tonneau, Algy Somerton pulled his goggles over his eyes and took the wheel, and a few moments later the big roadster was backed out. Goulokos had already signalled that the road was empty, so Algy lost no time in turning, and drove slowly along while the Greek ran ahead and opened the gates.

From what has been said of what took place in the cell at the convocation house, it will have been gathered that the Three Musketeers were determined on pulling off one more coup before making their getaway.

Had it not been for the report they had received from Abdul that same morning, it is a question whether they would have risked another stroke or not. They were no fools, and they did not need any telling just how much they had stirred up the activities of the Paris Sûreté, as well as every commissariat of police round about Paris.

They knew only too well that every gendarme in every department of the Seine valley was on the look-out for the three bandits who had been terrorising the countryside, and if it came to a show-down, it was good betting that the notorious Bonnet and his gang would have looked like small game compared to the fight the Three Musketeers were prepared to put up.

The killing of Coignet, of the Sûreté, had been a mistake, but at the time it had seemed to them a necessity. They knew, each of them, that this act would cause the Prefect in Paris to redouble his efforts to track them down, and that once they were located, the attack would come swiftly —an attack in which neither side could expect to receive or give quarter.

At the same time, there were no more desperate criminals living than those three young men who were known as the Three Musketeers; and whatever the reason was, devil-may-care daring, sheer bravado or actual criminal lust, they had decided on pulling off one more coup before clearing off with the spoil they had already accumulated.

If they had only known that the Senegalese who had created the disturbance at the inn on the island that morning had been sent down from Paris specially to do just what he had done, it would have put a very different complexion on matters. But they had accepted Abdul's report at face value, and they did not guess for a single moment that, after the arrest of the black, he had been quietly shunted back to Paris.

Nor did they dream that the man they had seen on the river bank by the washhouse float the previous evening, the man whose presence had contributed to their abandonment of the pursuit of the elusive black who had given them such a chase, was other than some casual pedestrian who had happened accidentally to be there at that time.

And certainly they did not guess that it could have been Sexton Blake, the famous London criminologist, who, above all other detectives, they wished least to find on their trail. But they did not know these things, nor even guess them. And they did not know that, aside from being at the inn on the island during the fracas that morning, Sexton Blake was even then in a punt just above the bridge.

They knew from what Abdul had said that a stranger, whom he had noticed twice at the inn, was in a punt fishing, but they had nothing whatsoever to connect this person with Sexton Blake.

So it was with the conviction that, so far, the Prefecture was at a dead end, they drove out of the grounds of the villa owned by Mathew Cardolak and took their way down past the abbey and the church, and through a narrow, old, cobbled street at the back of the church to main street, coming out just at the corner where it turned up from the western side of the town hall.

It has already been seen, from what has been written, that, just as in parts of England, it is the custom for big banks to have branches in small towns where the amount of business does not warrant keeping open every day in the week. And there are many such small places round about Paris where this system operates.

In a town the size of Poissy in England it would pay to keep two or three banks open on each business day, but in France, the average citizen (and more particularly in the country) is chary of banking institutions, and usually keeps his savings tucked away in an old sock concealed in the middle of a mattress, or some other hiding-place. Therefore, it has been found that a couple of days in the week is sufficient to handle what banking business there is, and it was just this knowledge on which the Three Musketeers were working. They had done it once before in the case of a small branch bank on the other side of the forest of St. Germain, and they figured what had worked once ought to work again.

They had chosen their time well. Like most places in France, the shops of Poissy are closed from mid-day until two in the afternoon, and the Three Musketeers had figured on arriving at the branch bank, which was their objective, just a few minutes before twelve, when the funds would have been collected ready for locking up during the two hours of closing.

The branch in question was situated just near the bend where they came out into the main street. Straight ahead of them the main road ran on past the Mairie, and under the railway bridge already referred to, to the bridge and the road which turned to the right, past the hotel known as Esturgeon, and that where Blake was staying.

Off to the right, another road ran to Maisons-Laffitte, while again to the left was a local street, which took one round to the lower end of the strand, and came out near the small railway bridge there, not far from the part of the river-bank where Tinker had lain in the grass the night before and told Blake what had occurred. The main road which turned the corner there was, of course, the road to Paris.

All these things had been carefully borne in mind by the Three Musketeers in their plan, and it had already been agreed that they would make their getaway by the Maisons-Laffitte road, which seemed to offer a better chance than the main road to Paris, for the former was wide and fairly straight for some distance, whereas the latter was narrow, and wound uphill past the shop, with the added complication of a tramway track.

Thus when he had driven into the main road, Algy Somerton, having come downhill, found himself placed wrong for a quick dash into the road to Maisons-Laffitte. He drove round in a circle, which took him right past the end of the Mairie and not fifty yards from the local commissariat, and then pulled into the kerb just in front of the small bank which was their objective.

Scarcely had the car come to a stop before Archie Pherison was out, followed by Reggie Fetherston. Algy Somerton sat at the wheel, the engine running, and his hands held loosely, ready for instant action the moment his accomplices should emerge. That was his part of the job, and from his appearance one would think he had not the slightest interest in what was transpiring inside the bank. But from the instant the two Musketeers had entered, things had begun to happen, and were continuing to do so.

The staff consisted of a senior clerk from the head office in Paris, assisted by a junior. They were both behind the counter, which stretched from one wall to the other, and admittance behind which was gained by a hinged section in the counter.

The right-hand part of the counter was enclosed by a wire grill, and both the senior and the junior were at that moment standing there checking up bundles of notes before placing them in the safe —just as the Three Musketeers had figured they would be doing.

Besides the two Musketeers there was one other person in the place, a man who looked like a local business man who had evidently been either depositing or drawing out money, and was now ready to depart.

Archie Pherison and Fetherston moved slowly, giving him a chance to go, and for a few seconds Pherison fumbled at an inner pocket, as if seeking his pocket-book.

But the moment the customer was through the door the two bandits came into action like a flash. Archie Pherison jerked out his automatic, and before the senior in charge had grasped what he was about, he found himself gazing into the blued muzzle.

At the same time Reggie Fetherston kicked open the hinged section of the counter, and, with his pistol also drawn, made for the grill.

The junior had fallen back with a terrified squeak at the sight of the pistols; but not so the senior. Despite the menace of that blued muzzle, he made a dive beneath the desk for his own weapon, and, clawing at it frantically, threw himself sideways, pulling the trigger as he fell.

It was a brave action, and just what many another man would have done in defence of the funds entrusted to his care. But it had not a hope of succeeding.

Before he could steady himself to aim properly, Archie Pherison pulled the trigger of his automatic —just once, and the senior, with his own smoking pistol still clutched in his hand, swung round and went down with a thud.

He struggled a few moments in a frantic effort to twist round and shoot again, but before he could do so Archie Pherison shot again, and this time the poor fellow lay still.

As for the junior, he was on his knees on the floor, shaking like a dry leaf, and, out of contempt, neither Pherison nor Fetherston took the trouble to shoot. Reggie Fetherston was already at the counter behind the grill, and while Archie Pherison kept guard on the door, he piled bundle after bundle of notes of denominations of thousand, five hundred, and hundred into his pocket until the counter was clear.

He made a hurried visit to the safe, where he found more loot, and then, with all the visible cash stuffed into his pockets, he gave a sign to Archie Pherison and made for the hinged section of the counter.

Pherison still stood guard while Fetherston went out through the door and jumped into the car; then Archie Pherison followed, and while his foot was still on the running-board, while the neighbouring shopkeepers, having heard the sound of the shots, were just running out, and while a distant gendarme was ambling along towards the scene of the commotion, Algy Somerton threw in the clutch, and the big roadster shot along the Maisons-Laffitte road like a thunderbolt.

The hold-up had gone absolutely according to schedule, and the police had one more score to mark up against the three bandits who worked as if they held them in utter contempt.

•　　•　　•　　•　　•

It will be recalled that, early that morning, Tinker, in obedience to Blake's instructions, left Poissy on the early morning train. It was the first train of the day for Paris, but Tinker did not proceed that far.

On the contrary, he descended at the very next station, which was Acheres, a large and important junction on the main trunk line, which is situated right at the edge of the forest of St. Germain.

It must be remembered that he was still in the disguise of an Indian student, and it was in order to get rid of this and assume another, that he was making for a secluded part of the forest.

On climbing down at Acheres with his bag, he walked leisurely along the platform to the gates, finding as he did so that he was apparently the only passenger to alight. He gave up his ticket and made his way to the road, where a brief survey showed him that if he wished to reach the forest by the shortest route, it would be necessary for him to cut across several lines of rails.

There was a chance that he might be held up in his progress by some of the railway hands, but he knew France well enough to be perfectly aware that most of the regulations in force in that country are made to be broken if they become onerous to the public, so he took a chance on the trespass. Moreover, at that hour of the morning there were not many persons about, even though Acheres was an important junction.

He found his calculations justified, for he got across the maze of tracks without being challenged, although as he passed one signal-box a man at the shunting levers glanced inquiringly at him. But Tinker kept on without a word, and the yard hand was evidently too busy to follow up his curiosity with a question.

Once across the tracks, Tinker had still to negotiate the engine-yard, where he saw more than two score engines standing by, ready for duty. He skirted these, passed behind the roundhouse, and then, crossing another road, found himself close to the edge of the trees which meant the forest.

A short distance away he caught sight of a small group of men busy with saws and axes over a big tree which had been recently felled. Tinker gave the group a wide berth, and, as he came upon a narrow, well-trodden path which seemed to lead into the forest, he followed it.

He knew enough of the district to guess that the path was probably just one of the numerous criss-cross tracks that covered the place, and, if followed to its end, would likely bring him out at another side of the forest.

As a matter of fact that was exactly the case, but for the purpose he had in view Tinker knew he must get well away from a path that was at all frequently travelled. He walked along at a steady pace for a quarter of a mile or so, finding as he advanced that the trees got thicker and thicker, and knowing from this that he was undoubtedly getting deeper into the forest.

It was then he caught sight of another path leading off to the right. It did not appear to have been so well travelled, so he took it on a random chance.

It was of far more irregular course than the first, but that did not matter to Tinker. All he wanted was to get to a secluded spot where he could find water, and where there would be no chance of being seen by anyone passing through.

This path in its turn brought him, after a good ten minutes' walk, to one still narrower, which shot off at a tangent, and, with the same idea in his mind, Tinker took it.

It was then he began to see that he had come as he had wished, for this new path grew even narrower as he progressed, and some instinct told him that its twisting course would take him as nearly into the heart of the forest as he could get there.

The ground began to change a little now, too. He crossed more than one miniature ravine, and, on reaching a small stream, almost decided to choose a spot near there.

He would have done so but for another and wider path that crossed nearby, and, as it looked better travelled than the one he was following, he decided to push on further.

He covered what he guessed to be another quarter of a mile or so, and then came to another ravine. The trees here were not quite so dense, and a little distance away he could see what seemed to be a cart road of some sort. He walked around to examine it, and found that it did not seem to have been travelled for some time past.

As he stood there, he caught the sound of water tinkling close at hand, and on pushing through the trees, came upon another miniature ravine, at the bottom of which ran a tiny stream, low at that time of the year. He followed the ravine along for a hundred yards or so, and then as he came to a dense thicket he nodded his head as if satisfied.

"This will do," he muttered. "I couldn't find a better place."

With that he tossed his bag down and unlocked it. Before beginning to change he took out a packet of sandwiches which he had bought at a cafe near the station in Poissy, and while he rested munched them leisurely.

He was debating just how he should apparel himself when he had got rid of his present disguise, and realised that, while he had a sufficiently mixed lot of garments with him to serve until he should get back to Poissy, it would be necessary, on reaching Blake's room, to make some additions from what his master might have brought along with him. Of course, both Blake and Tinker always carried a reserve of garments when possible, and in their profession it was necessary to be able to make, at urgent moments, as many as half a dozen different combinations from just a few articles.

Tinker figured that his best plan would be to garb himself, as nearly as possible, after the fashion of a youth of the district, but the first preliminary was to get rid of the black stain, and that he knew was going to be no easy matter.

It had been put on to withstand all ordinary risks, and it would have taken a long time for ordinary soap and water to make any impression on it. That was why it had withstood the long immersion in the river the night before. But Tinker was prepared for that, and when he had finished his sandwiches he began to strip.

He took off every shred of clothing until he was wearing only his turban. Then he took from the bag a bottle full of a plain white liquid, with which he began to rub his body freely. He made application after application, until he had completely used up the contents of the bottle; then, while he stood about to let the liquid dry —thus by a chemical process doing its work —he hurled the empty bottle into a stony part of the ravine, where it smashed to atoms.

As soon as he was satisfied that his skin was dry enough he got out a cake of soap and a towel, and, after a cautious reconnoitering of his surroundings, made his way down to the stream.

He found a shallow pool where, by lying flat, it was possible to cover his whole body with water, and thus he lay for the space of ten minutes or so, every sense on the qui vive for suspicious sounds.

But nothing happened, and when he was satisfied that his body was well soaked, he sat up and began to lather himself from head to foot with the soap.

The transformation was magical. As the soft suds came into contact with his skin the black stain came away freely, and by the time he had finished his lathering and splashing there was not a single particle of the stain remaining.

When he was satisfied that this was so, Tinker dried himself with the towel and made his way back to where he had left his bag.

On looking at his watch he was surprised to find that it was almost mid-day. He had been longer than he thought coming through the forest, and he began to work more quickly, realising that he must get back to Blake without further delay. He began to select an odd garment here and there, until he had collected sufficient to serve as a temporary disguise. Then he donned them.

When he was finished, he put on a cap, the peak of which he drew well down over his eyes, and, that done, closed the bag in preparation for his departure. He had just locked it, and was looking round to see if he was leaving anything behind, when he heard the unmistakable sound of a motorcar not far away, and, as he listened, the sound grew more and more distinct.

"Coming this way," he muttered, as he withdrew more deeply into the thicket. "There is something queer about that. Fancy a motor-car here in the very heart of the forest, and there isn't any real road. But maybe it is some sort of portable sawmill, or something like that. Anyway, I will sit tight until it passes."

He dropped down flat and lay so he could see through the screen of bushes towards the lower part of the ravine. The sound of the car was very distinct now, and then suddenly it stopped. He crept forward a little until his scope of vision was extended, and lay watching in the direction from which he thought the sound had come.

He was still watching when he heard voices, and then abruptly three figures came into view, not twenty yards away from him. And as he saw them, it took every ounce of Tinker's control to keep from betraying himself, for in the three figures he recognised none others than the Three Musketeers. There could be no mistake about that, for at that moment Archie Pherison took off his hat, and Tinker could hear him plainly as he said:

"Hurry up now, you fellows; there is no time to be lost. Bring the stuff along, Reggie!"

Tinker saw Reggie Fetherston coming then with a big suitcase in his hand, and a second later Algy Somerton moved forward to where the other two stood. They sought about with their eyes for a little, and a cold chill went down Tinker's spine as he saw Archie Pherison look straight towards the thicket where he lay concealed. The bandit made as if to walk towards it, but just then Reggie Fetherston, who had been gazing towards a clump of bushes a little closer to where they were standing, said:

"This will do over here. Come on, you two."

The pair followed him to the thicket he had indicated, and then they disappeared. But they did not go far, for from where he lay Tinker could hear them talking in low tones as they proceeded with whatever purpose had brought them there to that spot in the heart of the forest of St. Germain.

Tinker dare not move. His only hope was to lie quiet and trust to luck that they would not discover him. Why they had come there he could not guess, but a little later he had his answer when, to his amazement, first one, then another and another monkish figure appeared from behind the thicket.

Then Tinker understood. His pulses were racing now, and every nerve was on the qui vive as he watched Reggie Fetherston move away with the suitcase and disappear from view.

Pherison and Somerton stood talking together for a few moments; then as a low whistle sounded, Pherison made a gesture, and Algy Somerton also disappeared.

There was a brief silence then, and Tinker was wondering what Fetherston and Somerton could be up to when he heard a voice lifted as if in warning, and the next instant Archie Pherison jumped to one side.

Tinker heard the sound of the engine, first racing, then settling down. Next came the noise of the gears, and a moment or so later a big green car came into view, heading straight towards the ravine, with Algy Somerton standing on the running-board, his hands on the steering-wheel. He clung to his perch until the front wheels were almost over the edge of the ravine, then he jumped off nimbly, leaving the car to go plunging down into the rocky stream below.

It struck with a terrific crash which smashed the whole front part of the chassis and the engine. There was a splintering of the body work as well, and for one brief space the car seemed to stand straight up on its nose. Then it toppled over with a thud, and lay a complete wreck. The Three Musketeers stood watching until the final crash, then they moved off.

Tinker lay absolutely still for a long ten minutes. He was taking no chances on them coming back, despite the fact that he figured they had gone for good. But at the end of that time he crawled out and crept cautiously down the bank to the bottom of the ravine where the wrecked car lay. He spent some time examining what was left of it, and as he came upon the secret of the different coloured veneer panels he gave a low whistle.

"So that is the explanation," he muttered. "I'll bet the guv'nor will be glad to know why the description of the car was always different in so far as the colour was concerned. Now just what is their game? Is it a get-away? They couldn't have chosen a better disguise for this country —monk's robes —Benedictine, I think. The guv'nor must know this, and know it just as quick as I can get the word to him. I'll have to risk running up against them, and make Poissy by the first train I can catch. There isn't anything here worth while taking along. The suitcase just contains the clothes they took off. And if the guv'nor wants the stuff, I can find the place again. Three monks —a smashed car —and it looks like a get-away. The guv'nor will have to move fast if he is going to upset their game."

And with that Tinker set off at a fast walk in the direction whence he had come, but he knew nothing then of the most recent outrage perpetrated by the Three Musketeers.

SEXTON BLAKE had spent most of the morning fishing. He did not see Abdul depart from the inn nor return, for the simple reason that the Nubian went by a way which was invisible to Blake. But even though his occupation was apparently an idle one, Sexton Blake's mind was extremely busy. On the way out from the bank of the river in the punt, he had taken a course that would let him drop down close to the fourth arch of the bridge, where Tinker had been clinging the previous night when surprised by the sudden appearance of the Three Musketeers.

In a way, the new trail began at that point, or, rather, on the edge of the revetment of the island, a few yards from the kerbing of the pier, for, according to Tinker, it was the silent arrival of a canoe that had first aroused his curiosity, and the actions of the single occupant that had given birth to his suspicions.

There was no doubt in Blake's mind that the Three Musketeers were prime factors in the death of Coignet of the Sûreté. The trail had been picked up by the man from the Sûreté, and, by a rare intuition, had been followed by him to that island abutting on the bridge at Poissy.

Coignet's report had come out of the void, so to say, to leave that one thread in the hands of others who would follow in his footsteps, and it was not mere coincidence that Tinker had picked it up so quickly. A day's delay, and they would have missed it. But they had reached Poissy in time, and, now that he had done what he could to erase any suspicions which might have been roused the previous night, Blake was making an effort to get things into some sort of sequence before taking the next step.

It is true that he was not in possession of very much to go upon, but it was sufficient to enable him to link up each outrage that had been committed with the three criminals known as the Three Musketeers, and to construct a rough history of their actions for some months past.

But it all filtered down to the one major point, that Coignet had tracked them as far as Poissy, and that they were still in that neighbourhood —or, at least, were up to a few hours since. Could it be argued that all along they had had their lair at Poissy, Blake asked himself. If so, did that mean that they had stored their loot in the same neighbourhood? Then where could that lair be?

There could be no doubt that the mysterious occurrence the night before would need a deal of explaining if it were to be ranked as an ordinary event. And by no stretch of the imagination could it be so. Tinker was not given to romancing, and Blake was prepared to accept literally every word the lad had said. That being so, he could but believe that, one after another, the Three Musketeers had appeared at the same spot within a few minutes of each other —one by canoe, one by way of the bridge, and the third from the inn on the island —and, in the same way, one after another, had disappeared beneath the surface of the water close to the revetment opposite the fourth pier of the bridge.

And, according to Tinker, they had remained beneath the surface far longer than was humanly possible. In that case, where had they been during that time? They could not have swum under the water to some other point, there to emerge, for Tinker must have seen them. And again, there was their equally mysterious reappearance at the very same spot where they had gone under.

Somewhere there, Blake felt, was the answer to that part of the riddle, if not to the rest of the problem. And it was this phase of it that was occupying his mind as he cast and cast and cast on the face of the sluggish current.

He did not propose taking any open steps during the day, but he was determined to do so that night, and, in the meantime, he would have Tinker where there was no risk of being overheard, and he could question the lad in more detail.

That was about the conclusion he had reached by the time he had pulled in a dozen brace of fair-sized fish, with a score or more of small goujons. And it was then, too, he noted by his watch that it was half-past eleven.

Thinking that it was getting on time for Tinker to be showing up at the Rendezvous des Pecheurs, Blake pulled in his line, and, after winding it up and unjointing his rod, he prepared to pull back to the float.

Now the stake at which he had moored the punt was fairly well out in the river, opposite the seventh pier, to be exact, and there the current ran freely. In addition to the stake at which he had moored, there were several score more, and as he gazed round he saw twenty odd other punts moored about him. He had noticed two or three punts drop away as their occupants gave it up for the time being, and in one or two instances he had seen them drift down under the arch of the bridge.

As there seemed nothing out of the ordinary in that, he decided to do the same, and when he had untied he took the oars and guided the craft easily while it slipped down on the current and underneath the seventh arch. But as soon as he was through, Blake set to work on the oars, and began pulling round so as to head for the bank just beneath the veranda cafe of the Esturgeon.

In order to make that spot, he had, of course, to pull past the lower end of the island on which the inn stood, and through the narrow race of water that ran between it and the two other islands that lay just below it. He was already prepared for the sweep of the current there, and a few strong strokes took him through.

But he made no attempt to stop at the Esturgeon float. Instead, he brought the nose of the punt upstream again, and rowed through just beneath the third arch, which took him close past the pier on the one side, and the spot where the Three Musketeers had disappeared on the other.

As the punt slipped through, he shot a glance first at the water-level kerbing of the pier, then at the revetment opposite, and finally at the ancient stone arching overhead. But not a sign of anything did he see to explain the mystery of the night before.

He pulled on to the other float above the bridge, where he had hired the punt, and, after paying the man, dropped his catch of fish into the creel, and set off for the Rendezvous des Pecheurs.

On reaching his own inn, Blake presented his catch to the proprietaire, who thanked him profusely and toddled off to the kitchen with them. Then Blake ascended to his room, where he found that Tinker had not yet put in an appearance. He washed up, and after a cigarette in the chair by the window —from where he could see and study again the island by the bridge —he went down to dejeuner.

He chose a table just inside the open door of the little restaurant and gave his order. The first dish —one of eggs —came in a few minutes, and he had just finished this, and was waiting for the second course of fish, when his ear caught the sound of loud shouting somewhere in the town. This did not rouse much curiosity at first, for he knew how volatile the French race is, and was quite aware that some perfectly mild subject of conversation might be the cause of the commotion.

But when the sounds grew louder, reaching a pitch which carried a note that one could hardly ignore, and when he saw several men running along the strand towards the corner by the Esturgeon, where the main road passed from the bridge, he grew more curious.

Then he saw the proprietors of his own inn rush out and question some men who were passing. They held an excited conversation for a few moments, and as the men ran on the proprietaire ran back in, jerking off his apron as he came, and yelling for his coat and hat.

Blake rose and followed him into the bar.

"What is it?" he asked, in his Norman patois.

"I don't know exactly, monsieur," returned the other, "but they do say there has been trouble at the bank. Shooting has been heard. I am going along to see."

"And I, too," muttered Blake.

He went back into the restaurant, where he had left his hat, and, telling the girl to keep the rest of his dejeuner until he returned, he joined the patron, and together they walked briskly in the direction of the corner. As they turned this, and came into the main street, they could see a lot of people running along in the direction of the far corner where the main street turned, and as they got still farther along they could see a dense crowd at that corner. They broke into a trot, and, passing down under the railway bridge, came up the slope to the level just in front of the town hall and mairie combined. It will be remembered that at one end of this same building was the commissariat of police, and as Blake glanced in that direction he saw several gendarmes rushing round the corner of the building. They did not pause, but kept on until they reached the fringe of the crowd, and just then Blake saw some men coming through the open door of the bank, carrying a prostrate form.

"It is the manager," he heard someone say. "He was shot, but they say he is not dead. They are taking him to the hospital."

"What has happened?" Blake heard the patron of his hotel ask someone else, and he stood close to listen to the reply.

"A hold-up," came the answer. "Just before the bank was closing, a big car stopped, and two men went in, while one remained in the car. They shot the manager, and took all the money they could lay their hands on —a very large sum, it is said. Then they rushed out and jumped in the car, which has gone off along the Maisons-Laffitte road. Ah, see, the police are going after it now. But they will never catch them. They never do."

Blake turned and looked in the direction which the man indicated. By the corner of the town hall was a big touring car, which the police had evidently commandeered. Into it half a dozen gendarmes were piling, and as the last one tumbled aboard the car went off with a roar along the Maisons-Laffitte road.

As it disappeared in a cloud of dust, Blake turned back to see what else was going on. They had now got the wounded bank official into a car, and in a few moments it, too, drove off in the direction of the local hospital. Then two other gendarmes emerged from the bank and turned the key in the door. What had become of the junior clerk, of whom he had heard some mention, he couldn't guess, but at that moment the lad was in the office of the commissaire, making a statement of what had occurred.

Blake looked at the patron of his hotel, and, seeing that he was engaged in talking with some friends, he took the opportunity to slip away and make for the commissariat.

As he reached the door and entered, he saw that the inner door of the commissaire's room was closed, and two gendarmes on duty in the outer room made as if to order him out. But before they could do so, Blake was across the office, and, after knocking, opened the door of the commissaire's room.

He saw that official at his desk, and a frightened-looking youth standing beside it. At that moment the two gendarmes grasped him by the arms and would have jerked him back roughly, but the commissaire looked up, and recognising Blake, made an imperative gesture, which caused the two astonished gendarmes to let go.

Without any word of explanation, Blake stepped into the room and closed the door. Then he approached the desk and accepted the chair to which the commissaire waved him. He sat there until the youth from the bank had completed his statement and was dismissed; then the commissaire turned a harassed look in his direction and said:

"You have heard, M. Blake?"

Blake nodded.

"I have just come from the bank," he said. "I have heard gossip, but should like to know exactly what has happened."

For answer the commissaire read the detailed statement which the youth had made, and added details, which had been given him by neighbouring tradesmen and casual pedestrians who had happened to be in the street when the hold-up took place. When he had finished, Blake nodded.

"The description of the car and the three men fits," he said. "It looks like the same trio we are seeking."

"It does, M. Blake —it does! They have got a clean start, and it will be difficult to overtake them. I have already telephoned to Acheres and Maisons-Laffitte to be on the watch for them. Can you make any suggestion?"

Blake shook his head.

"Not at the moment," he answered. "We shall have to wait and see what success your men have. But I shall think the thing over, monsieur, and if something occurs to me I shall communicate with you. I have been following up one line of investigation, but this may upset all my calculations. We shall see. Could you manage to get word to me at the Rendezvous des Pecheurs, if your gendarmes have any success?"

"I shall send a note round the moment I hear, M. Blake."

"Thank you! I do not think I had better be seen here more than is necessary. If I have something to communicate I shall get word to you somehow." And, with that, he got up and took his departure.

He passed through the outer room without a glance at the two mystified gendarmes, and, on reaching the road, managed to mingle again with the crowd, without attracting attention to himself, and, seeing that the patron of his inn was still engrossed with his friends, Blake made his way back to the inn, knowing that he could learn nothing more of value just then.

He finished his interrupted dejeuner, after which he ascended to his room and filled his pipe. He again seated himself by the window, and as he smoked gave his mind to this new problem which had arisen to complicate a case that was already sufficiently complex. It was, to his mind, almost a certainty that this latest brazen hold-up was the work of the same three bandits who had been operating for months in and about Paris.

And that, equally to Blake, meant the Three Musketeers. Their nerve was appalling when one looked at it. Whatever they had felt up to the time Coignet had appeared on the scene, they must have known then that the criminal investigation department of the Paris Sûreté was devoting every effort to the case. Their cold-blooded killing of Coignet proved that.

It was impossible for Blake to tell what they may have thought the previous night when they had pursued Tinker, but their actions were sufficient to reveal that they were very much on the alert. Blake could not help being puzzled, therefore, at this new outrage.

Were they so utterly contemptuous of the efforts of the police that they had committed this new crime, so close to their lair, merely to show that contempt? Or was it a last kick, so to speak, before they decamped. That was the point on which everything hinged, so far as Blake was concerned. In almost every respect, the hold-up was the same as the previous bank raid in which they had been implicated. It showed a careful planning, and on intimate knowledge of the bank routine.

Blake knew that the branch at Poissy was only open on two days each week, and he likewise realised that there would be likely to be more actual cash in the place on a Friday than on a Tuesday, for he knew that the local market was held on a Thursday. This, too, must have been known to the Three Musketeers.

He had no doubt that by now the local commissaire had advised the Prefecture in Paris of what had occurred, and from the Sûreté word would be sent broadcast for all police to be on the look-out for a car such as would be described.

Blake could do nothing in that direction. But he could try to figure out just what they would do next —where they would try to make for. He recalled that on other occasions what little trail they did leave had nearly always been in the direction of the forest of St. Germain. It was due to that that Coignet had eventually tracked them as far as Poissy. It looked to Blake like sheer madness for them to try and get into Paris in broad daylight after such a raid, when every gendarme for miles about would be on the watch for them.

There was no question that they had taken the Maisons-Laffitte road, and Blake's own knowledge told him that there were very few roads between Poissy and Paris where they could turn off, and only one between Poissy and Maisons-Laffitte, which would be too risky for them. If they had intended trying to make for the coast, then they must have taken another direction —that is over the bridge. And they had gone exactly opposite.

But there was the great forest of St. Germain between Poissy and

Maisons-Laffitte. In that vast range of woodland there were many, many secluded spots where one could hide, and, as he viewed the thing from all angles, Blake came to the conclusion that it was the forest for which they would make.

Once well inside it, they could make in a dozen different directions, and if they parted company, each man going on his own, they stood a fair chance of slipping through any cordon, for no net could yet be spread that would cover more than a very small part of the possible exits from the forest.

From what has already been seen of Tinker's movements, it will be understood just how correct Blake's system of thinking was; but even his trained mind did not penetrate the problem far enough to guess just how the fugitives would emerge from the forest. And he was still smoking and pondering the problem when there came the sound of footsteps outside the door and a knock.

Blake called a command to enter, and the next instant the handle turned, and a young man of the local type stepped into the room. He carefully closed the door after him and locked it. Then he came across, and, after tossing his cap aside, sat on the edge of the bed. Blake had nodded, and was now looking at him critically.

"Not so bad a change," he said at last. "You might have made one or two additions, and you can find some things in my luggage."

"I'll do that later, guv'nor," said the lad. "I just got in —caught a train that got here a few minutes before two. I've got great news, guv'nor; but first I want to ask you what has happened here. There are crowds all along the main street, and, as I came along, from what I could gather, there seems to have been a hold-up here."

Blake nodded.

"There has," he answered. "A rotten hold-up at the bank. It looks like the Three Musketeers again —two of them went into the bank just a few minutes before midday and shot the visiting manager —got away with a big sum, I believe —escaped in a car along the Maisons-Laffitte road. Gendarmes have gone after them, and the alarm has been telephoned broadcast, but they got away with a good start. I have been trying to figure out where they could, or would make for. I can only think of the forest of St. Germain."

Tinker gave an excited exclamation.

"You are right on that, guv'nor," he said. "I can tell you just where they went, and what they did after they escaped. I didn't know what they had been up to, but what you tell me fits in all the pieces of the puzzle. And I can give you a pretty good idea where they are at this very moment."

"You!" exclaimed Blake. "What do you mean, my lad?"

"Listen, sir."

Then briefly, but missing no important, detail, Tinker related all that had happened from the time he had left Poissy on the early train that morning until he had seen the Three Musketeers come into the forest of St. Germain in the green roadster; told how they had donned the robes of monks, and had wrecked the car in the bottom of the ravine.

"As soon as I thought it was safe I went after them," he proceeded from that point. "I found it easy enough to pick up their trail, but you may be sure, sir, I kept well out of sight. They went towards Acheres, almost the way I had come into the forest from there; but they did not go as far as the railway station. I did not know just what was the best thing to do then. Of course, I knew nothing about this hold-up at the bank here, and I couldn't guess what they were up to. Anyway, I dodged about the edge of the forest until I saw them on the road, and I risked following them a bit until it looked certain that they were walking back this way."

"Do you mean towards Poissy?"

"Yes, guv'nor. They took the Poissy road. Well, then I thought my best hunch was to get a train back, if there was one soon, and so I made for the station. Thank goodness, there are frequent trains down from Paris at this time of the day, and I hadn't to wait long. But that is not all, sir. Just after we left Poissy, the train ran —as you probably know it does —for some distance close to the road, and as we went along I saw my three Benedictine monks in a big farm-cart —an empty one. You know the sort, guv'nor, that goes into the Paris markets from the vegetable-growing districts round about Paris. This one looked as if it might be on its way back from a trip to Paris, and had overtaken the three monks, and had given them a lift. That is all, guv'nor, except what I have told you about what I heard along the street as I made my way here from the station. Now, what do you think it all means, guv'nor?"

Blake did not answer at once. He was gazing out of the window across towards the inn on the island, pondering on what the lad had told him. For a good ten minutes he sat thus, then his gaze travelled slowly along from the island to the fourth arch of the bridge, from there to the massive piers and the heavy stone topping of the structure, and finally it swept back until the end of the bridge was concealed by the bulk of the Esturgeon. Finally, he turned his head and looked at Tinker.

"What you have just told me is the biggest and most important contribution we have had in this case since we tackled it, my lad. It is of prime importance —every word of it. You did exactly right back in the forest. To have risked more would have been to court discovery, and discovery would have been fatal. We still have a chance. It is as I thought. Those three criminals feel so sure of their ground, or so contemptuous of the police that they have brought off this latest coup in sheer bravado. But they have over-reached themselves this time. We must clinch that. They are returning to Poissy for just one reason —because they are not quite ready to make a getaway. But they will try to go soon, Tinker. Every instinct I have tells me that. And we must snaffle them before they can get clear. They must not be allowed to get into that forest again. If they do, they will give us the slip.

"All the morning a certain idea has been growing in my mind. This afternoon, I am going to test it. If there is anything in it, then it will not take me long to plan our next step. If it fizzles out, then we shall have to think up something else. But, in the meantime, there is work for you to do. Get what you need out of my luggage, then go downstairs and take some food. When you have done that, make for the outer part of the town —along the Maisons-Laffitte road —and watch for those three monks. If you can pick them, up, stick to them until you see where they go to earth. And when you do come back here, if I am not here, wait for me."

And with that Blake knocked the ashes from his pipe, and rose, his movements telling the lad as plainly as words that he was bent on some definite purpose.

CHAPTER 13. In Which Sexton Blake Visits the Library — Seeking the Assistance of the Commissaire of Police —The Detective's Plans.

ON leaving his inn, Sexton Blake made his way into the main street of the town and walked along until he reached the town hall. He entered the building, and after making certain inquiries, was directed to a room on the upper floor. He ascended the staircase, and, after some examination of numerous closed doors there, found the one he sought. He knocked, and entered a room that was about as uninteresting in appearance as one could imagine.

It was a large apartment, of which the walls were completely covered by plain wooden shelves reaching the whole way from floor to ceiling. In the main body of the room were several plain deal tables, on which reposed piles and piles of dusty papers and books, quite yellow with age.

There was a single human occupant of the room, seated behind a table in the very midst of the disorder. He was a shrunken little old man, whose appearance seemed strangely in keeping with that of the room, and who at the moment was engaged in the perusal of a heavy tome, which he was holding close to weak eyes which were reinforced with large horn spectacles.

So engrossed was he in his occupation that he had heard neither Blake's knock nor entry, and it was not until the visitor had traversed half the length of the room and was standing close to the table at which he sat that he became aware of his presence.

Then he gave a jump and a little squeak. He looked up and shot out an irritable question as to what the visitor wanted, for it was rarely indeed that anyone took the trouble to invade that room. It was where all the municipal archives of the town were kept, and Blake knew that at the time of the expulsion of the Roman church from France a few years ago, a great many of the church and abbey archives had been taken there.

As for the books and papers relating to the town, they had been laid away there during several centuries, and it was only on rare occasions that the solitary guardian was disturbed. Hence his start and irritation at the intrusion, for the little old man had been dreaming away his days among his dusty charges for more than half a century, and in that time he had grown almost as dry and dusty as his charges.

But Blake knew from long experience just how to handle persons of that type, and how to get them interested; and inside ten minutes he had brought the librarian into a very different frame of mind. Judiciously he brought the conversation round where he wanted it, and soon after the two of them were deep in a discussion of the mediaeval history of Normandy in general, and Poissy in particular.

Of course, Blake was still dressed in the somewhat rough garments in which he had first come to Poissy, but he soon convinced the guardian of the archives that he was a substantial Norman citizen from near Rouen, and the real knowledge he showed of ancient history was all the introduction the other really needed. They talked for the better part of an hour, and gradually Blake drew out the information he was after.

At the end of that time, the librarian was in the mood to do everything in his power to make his visit an interesting one, and when Blake finally asked to be permitted to examine some of the old documents dealing with the church and the abbey, the little guardian was only too pleased to dig up what he wanted.

Then Blake settled down at another table, and by the time another half-hour had passed, he had sorted out the various documents until he had a dozen or so which, he thought, might prove of interest. So he concentrated on these.

By this time the librarian had returned to his own tome, almost forgetting the existence of his visitor, and for the next two hours the silence of the room was only broken by the slow tick-tock of the old clock in the corner, an occasional cough, and the rustling of the pages of the tome or the sheets of papers which Blake was studying.

As he proceeded with his investigation of the documents, Blake, as was his habit when studying anything, began to classify what he found, and at the end of two hours he had brought his study down to three general categories —one was a history of the cathedral as the old papers showed it; the second was a history of the abbey; and the third covered several fragments of old papers relating to Queen Blanche, the mother of St. Louis, and that lady's activities during the time she had lived at Poissy.

On these three he concentrated, and it was not until nearly six o'clock that he finally gathered the documents together and rose.

He thanked the librarian profusely for his kindness, and received from that gentleman an invitation to come in again at any time during his stay in the place.

Then Blake took his departure, but instead of making his way back to his inn, he made his way to the river-bank above the bridge, and seated himself on the turf there, he filled his pipe, and, when it was going well, he sat studying the fragment of the building at the end of the bridge, which it was said was part of the old mill which had originally been built by Queen Blanche.

Next he gave his attention to the piers of the bridge one after the other until he came to the fourth, against which the island on which the Nubian's inn stood abutted. But his chief attention was given to the heavy, deep stonework above the piers which formed the main highway of the bridge, and for the first time Sexton Blake found something to remark in the extraordinary depth of that stonework.

After a time he rose, and making his way back to the approach of the bridge, walked out on it. He continued on past the island until he reached the middle, and then, turning, he found that he could see over the roofs close to the bank and along to the two steeples of the cathedral on the hill beyond.

He followed several imaginary lines with his eye, and the more he did so the more he became inwardly convinced that there might be something in the idea which had inspired him to visit the room containing the old archives, and which had been decidedly strengthened from what he had read there.

He walked back to the Rendezvous des Pecheurs, and, on ascending to his room, found Tinker had returned. When Blake had closed the door, he looked inquiringly at the lad, and Tinker nodded.

"It was the right hunch, guv'nor," he said, in a low tone. "I picked them up all right just as they were entering the town, and I tracked them to the point where they went to earth."

"Where was it?" asked Blake quickly.

"You know the old abbey, sir?"

"Yes, of course."

"Well, it was there. I'll explain, guv'nor. They didn't come into the town by the Maisons-Laffitte road, but turned off before they got to the boundaries and came through by the market place. From there they took a course by several winding streets, until they came out by the church, and then crossed the open space and passed under the outer gate-arch of the old abbey. I went after them at a little distance, and as the cobbled lane inside the old gate twists a good deal, it wasn't very hard to keep their trail. Well, sir, they went through an old garden there and into a stone building.

"I didn't dare go any closer, but I met a man on my way out, and professed to be very interested in the abbey. I asked him several questions, and finally got him to tell me what the old stone building was which they entered. He said it was the old convocation house, whatever that may mean, and was one of the only two buildings which still remained in the possession of the church. I thought I had better not ask any more then, so I thanked him and came away. But, anyway, there it is, guv'nor —the Three Musketeers, for what it may be worth, are disguised as three Benedictine monks, and they are now —or were half an hour ago —in what is known as the convocation house of the old abbey."

"You have given me the last link, my lad," said Blake, when Tinker had finished. "I can't go into detailed explanations now, but while I was fishing this morning I formed a certain tentative theory which was strengthened by a visit I paid to a room in the town-hall this afternoon where the old town and church archives are kept. After that, I took a bit of a stroll, and from certain general measurements and directions which I took, I found nothing to make me abandon that theory. It all depended on one or two things, and one of those you have given me just now. Only events will show whether I am right or wrong; but this night, my lad —this night after it is dark, we are going to test that theory, and before we are finished we shall know the truth, not only of certain things which took place in mediaeval times, but also of what is vastly more important to us —the secret of the Three Musketeers.

"I cannot but believe that they will try to get away from here soon now. They have everything to gain by doing so, and everything to lose by remaining. I propose taking every step in my power to catch them in the net to-night, and I am going off now to see the local commissaire. If we fail —if my theory is a false one, then we shall achieve nothing. On the contrary, we shall probably find ourselves the object of considerable amusement on the part of the local gendarmerie here. But that is a risk we must take. There are a few points at which I wish gendarmes posted before we set to work, and after that it will be up to us. So get some food and hold yourself in readiness. I shall be back ere long."

And with that Blake once more left the inn.

His first visit was to the commissaire of police, but on inquiring for that official he was informed that he had gone home. Blake trudged along to his residence, and, although the commissaire was at his evening meal, he at once took Blake into his study. He informed the detective that so far no traces had been found of the three fugitives who had robbed the local bank, but of course Blake knew more about their movements than the police official.

Then he broached the object of his visit, and although the commissaire evinced deep curiosity to know just what Blake had in mind, the detective did not enlighten him entirely, and in view of the cards which the Prefect in Paris had given Blake, the local official could not refuse his request.

Blake's principal request was for a force of gendarmes to be placed at his disposal, and as Poissy is the chief gaol town for that district, there could be, he knew, no difficulty in assembling as many as he thought would serve his purpose. That point settled, he sat down and jotted on a sheet of paper just where he wished them placed in various groups, some points requiring, he thoughts as few as two, while at others he asked for as many as five to be placed. The hour he set at eight o'clock, and when this was settled he made to depart.

"Will you wish to keep in touch with me?" asked the commissaire as he rose.

Blake nodded.

"Most, certainly, monsieur," he answered tactfully. "It would be better if you could spare the time to take personal charge of the force."

"You can depend on that then, M. Blake," was the rejoinder. "I shall personally see that the men are at their posts, and I shall remain in my office all the evening until I hear from you. If you really think you will be able to flush these criminals here to-night, fear not, they shall not escape. But, you will pardon me, I think you are wrong. In my opinion, they are far away from Poissy by now, and will not return here. They would not dare."

"To-night will show," said Blake pleasantly. "My theory may be all wrong, but with your permission, monsieur, we shall give it a test."

And with that he left.

At exactly half-past eight that evening the next step, after the placing of the gendarmes, was accomplished. This was the quiet roping in of Abdul the Nubian. At that hour a force of five gendarmes visited the inn on the island and arrested him, and so little notice did they attract that scarcely a soul was aware of what had happened.

By this time the other groups had been placed as Blake wished. There were three gendarmes on duty at the far end of the bridge, four at the Poissy end, two inside the old abbey gate and two outside, four at the edge of the town on each of the four main roads leading from it both in the direction of Paris and elsewhere, and another half-dozen or so at the commissariat under the direction of the commissaire ready as reinforcements whenever required.

In addition, there were three more with a sort of roving commission, whose duty it was to patrol the bank of the river between the bridge and the lower end of the strand.

And it says a good deal for the care taken by the commissaire that each group had taken up post without arousing undue curiosity on the part of the inhabitants. But, of course, before ten o'clock the town would be pretty well in bed, and even at nine there were but few pedestrians about.

At a quarter to nine Sexton Blake and Tinker quietly left the Rendezvous des Pecheurs. They walked across the strand, keeping well under cover of the trees, and made their way down an old stone flight of steps close to the veranda of the Esturgeon. On reaching the bank, Blake led the way to the Esturgeon float, where he coolly commandeered a light rowing skiff. They both climbed in, and Tinker pulled across to the revetment at the island, where one of the Three Musketeers had tied the canoe the previous night.

It was dark by now and would remain so for an hour at least before the waxing moon cleared the trees to the east. When the nose of the skiff touched the stone revetment, Tinker caught hold, and held it while Blake slipped off his outer clothes. Then he stepped across the gunwale and stood on the edge of the revetment.

He knew what he was going to do and so did Tinker. They had discussed the thing in every detail, and had finally come to the conclusion that the only way to find out what had become of the Three Musketeers when they had disappeared beneath the surface of the water the night before was to follow the same procedure.

It was both literally and figuratively a leap in the dark, and neither of them knew what the result might be. But it was all part of Sexton Blake's theory; and tucked away in his mind was a suspicion of what he might come upon.

While he held on with one hand Tinker took out his automatic with the other, and then Blake slipped easily into the water, and after hanging on by his fingers for a moment or two, suddenly let himself sink. Tinker bent forward, watching the surface of the water intently. The seconds dragged past slowly until he had mechanically counted sixty. A minute, then another sixty, and he knew if Blake were beneath there groping about he must soon break the surface. But he counted off a third minute and still Blake did not show, and when a fourth minute had gone by Tinker began to get anxious.

Five and six and seven minutes passed, and by then Tinker knew that Blake had either come upon what he had suspected he might or else he had become entangled among the weeds at the bottom, and would never appear until he were found by the drag hooks.

But all of a sudden, while these thoughts were passing through his mind, the surface close to the skiff was broken, and Blake's dark head appeared. He gripped the edge of the revetment and drew himself up, then he bent over until he could whisper to Tinker.

"The first trick is ours, my lad. I found exactly what I suspected might exist. We will start from this end. Tie the skiff and follow me. The next move is from the cellar of the inn on this island."

While Tinker did as he was bid, Blake slipped back into his outer clothes, and then led the way through the densely shaded garden to the side door of the inn. Since the arrest of Abdul, the place had been closed to custom, and a gendarme had been left in charge.

In response to Blake's low knocking he opened the door a trifle, and then as Blake gave the password, which had been agreed upon between him and the commissaire, the man swung the door wide and permitted them to enter.

In a few words Blake explained that they were going into the cellar, and warned the man to be on his guard until they should reappear.

Then they went down the stairs into the cellar, which they knew must be considerably below the normal level of the river, and as the gendarme closed the door after them, Blake brought his electric-torch into play. He seated himself on a case of beer, and motioned for Tinker to come close. The lad leant against a cask of wine, and when he had got a cigarette going Blake said:

"There is no great hurry. I don't want to get into action too early, and it is only about nine o'clock. If we reach our destination by half-past nine it will be in good time."

"But what is our destination, guv'nor?" asked Tinker. "I know, something of what you have figured out, but I don't understand what we are in this cellar for, and how this is going to take us to the Three Musketeers."

Blake smiled and rose.

"Hold the torch," he ordered.

And when Tinker had taken it, he walked across to the wall which abutted on to the bridge and worked away there for some time dragging down cases of bottles and placing them to one side. When he had cleared a wide space, he motioned to Tinker to bring the torch closer, and then as his hand followed the course of certain lines in the stone, Tinker's eyes opened wide.

"A door!" he gasped.

"Exactly," said Blake, "and just what I expected to find. We will go through in a few minutes; but I will tell you first what I have discovered, and just what we are about to do. I got my theory out of my own head while fishing this morning. It was inspired by what I already knew of the customs of mediaeval times, when practically every abbey and monastery and convent and castle was honeycombed with secret passages, as a means of hiding or escape in times of stress. It was customary with us in England as well. And this afternoon I came on certain references among the old archives at the town hall which convinced me I was right. Now listen."

CHAPTER 14.   *The Passage Under the Town —Run to Earth — Conclusion.*

SEXTON BLAKE then explained to Tinker how, bit by bit, from the old documents, he had pieced together enough to give him a fairly complete history of the old abbey, the church, the convent, the bridge and Queen Blanche's mill from the earliest times.

He told how he found several veiled references to a secret underground passage, and, piece by piece, he had traced that out until he found that it ran from the abbey to the church, thence along to a deep cellar beneath the convent, and from there to the mill at the end of the bridge which, in Blake's opinion, had been erected merely as a blind, and in order to keep that section of the secret passage in control of the proper hands.

Then he asked the lad if he had noticed how very deep the top stonework of the bridge was, and when Tinker replied that he had, Blake said:

"I figured out this afternoon that there would be plenty of room there for a passage if the original builders had wanted to make one, and then it all came to me how easy it would be for a fugitive from either abbey or church or convent to escape during persecuted times by a secret passage to the bridge, and from the bridge by way of this island to a boat in the river. Well, my lad, when I looked up the history of this inn and found that the island had also formed part of the church domain, and that the original building here had been a so-called house of retreat used by the monks, I figured I was on the right track.

"And now I can tell you what became of the Three Musketeers last night. When they disappeared beneath the surface they went down for some eight or nine feet, and then by working their way in under the revetment they came up to the surface inside the fourth pier of the bridge —that is the one against which this island abuts. It is almost hollow. It is a very large pier, as you have seen, and the inside is almost as large as a small room. There are two ledges there, and against each side a door. One, I feel sure, connects with this door in front of us by a passage, and the other with the main secret tunnel which should lead clear through to the abbey, and, unless it comes out somewhere in that convocation house of which you told me, then I miss my guess very badly.

"For the rest, there is nothing but water inside the pier, but, of course, plenty of air room above, for the open space is vaulted, and, even at flood level, the water would not be above the two ledges. There is a plank from one ledge to the other, and I think we shall eventually discover that it has been used very recently. I can understand now why Abdul was planted here at the inn. It gave the Three Musketeers complete control of both ends of the secret passage. It is a question if anyone now living in Poissy knows anything about the old passage, unless it be the old man in charge of the archives. When the sewerage system is extended here, they will probably come on the secret, and then everyone will know of it, but, so far, I believe, it is known only to us and the Three Musketeers.

"I don't know how they found out about it, but that doesn't matter. Now you understand, my lad, and it is time we were making a move."

"You mean we are going to try and get through to the old abbey from here, guv'nor?" asked Tinker, "right under the town?"

"Just that, my lad. If the birds are flown, then the gendarmes on duty at the abbey ought to succeed in roping them in. Every gendarme on duty to-night has the description of them as they would appear in ordinary clothes, and as you saw them in monkish, robes this afternoon. But I am hopeful that we shall be able to jump them before they make a start. Now, let us get busy." And, suiting the action to the word, Blake rose, tossed away the end of his cigarette and addressed himself to the rectangular block of stone in the wall which he figured was nothing more or less than a door.

Blake had spent a good deal of time in studying old mediaeval ruins, and he knew pretty well the general principle adopted in the building of secret passages and closets, he knew if the block of stone in front of him was a door, then it ought to work on the pivotal principle, and once he discovered the point of pivotal pressure it ought to yield.

And it took him less than ten minutes to read the riddle. As the great block swung on its pivot Tinker held the torch close, and through the opening they could see a low, dark passage.

Blake took the torch and led the way through, and as he went along he kept the light trained ahead. They had gone less than thirty feet when the bright beam showed what looked like a wall of stone ahead, and a few moments later they walked out on the stone ledge which Blake had seen when he had dived under the revetment and had come up inside the hollow pier. He swung the light round so that Tinker could see the whole chamber, and then with a sign to the lad to follow, he crossed the plank which connected with the other ledge.

The door opposite, like the one giving on to the ledge they had just left was partly ajar, and, after pausing a few seconds so that Tinker could look down at the surface of the water a few feet beneath and understand just how the whole place had been arranged, Blake pushed the second door open, revealing another passage, so low that they had to bend half double to negotiate it. They went along this for what seemed a considerable distance, and then the roof gradually sloped up until they could stand upright with ease.

Blake paused.

"We have reached the end of the bridge," he whispered. "We are right under the house which is a fragment of the old mill. You can see the passage ahead. It ought to take us on to the convent, and then, if I am right, we should find that it branches, one branch leading to some place beneath the church and the other to the abbey. Come on now, my lad, and make as little noise as possible. Keep your pistol handy, for we don't know what we are going to strike at the other end."

Once more Blake took the lead, and they went along the narrow chilly passage which seemed first to dip down for a considerable distance, then to begin to ascend. From the way it went Blake was figuring just what course they were following, and suddenly, when they came out into a small square stone-walled room he paused again and pointed towards a door on the right.

"That will lead into the convent cellars," he whispered. "Our way is still on."

Once more they proceeded, and then, still ascending, they came to what Blake had said he expected to find —a point where the passage spilt into two, one leading off to the right and the other to the left.

"The left-hand passage to the church, the right-hand to the abbey," he muttered, as if repeating a formula.

He took a glance to see that Tinker had his weapon ready, then he started on and, after a few yards, the passage bent again sharply to the right. After a little, however, it grew straight, and then, when they had covered another fifty yards or so, the beam of the electric torch revealed another stone door ahead. At sight of it Blake halted, and bent close to Tinker.

"Beyond that door we shall know," he whispered. "Watch every step, my lad. Be on the qui vive, for you know the calibre of those three criminals, and if you have to shoot, then shoot to make every bullet tell."

Tinker nodded his understanding, and with infinite caution Sexton Blake began to traverse those last few yards of stone passage towards the door that lay between them and —what?

As he reached the door Blake switched off the torch and laid a cautioning hand on the lad's arm. Together they stood close to the door listening, but either the stone was too thick and fitted too tightly, or there was no one on the other side, for they could hear nothing.

Blake thrust the torch into his hip-pocket and began feeling along beside the door until he found what he sought. He kept pressing gently all the time, and suddenly he felt the stone swing away from him under his weight, he pushed it steadily until a cold draught of air struck them, and then he thrust his head and shoulders through the opening.

As he did so he caught the gleam of a line of light almost opposite, and knew that it came through a partly-open door. Listening, he heard the sound of a boot heel on stone, and then the murmur of voices reached him.

And now he knew that beyond that half-open door there were human beings talking. Had he at last found the lair of the Three Musketeers?

He drew back and placed his lips close to Tinker's ear. He breathed a few words and then, holding his automatic in his right hand, he squeezed through the opening with the lad close at his heels.

On reaching the other side Blake paused a moment, then he tip-toed towards the vertical shaft of light until he could peer through into the next apartment. And it was then he saw, in the cell-like place the figures of three monks, seated on truckle beds and smoking and talking just as if they were having an ordinary evening's chat together.

But at that second it seemed as if some prescience of danger reached Archie Pherison, for he broke off suddenly in what he was saying and turned his head towards the half-open door.

To Blake it seemed that the bandit must have seen them, but then it appeared not, for Archie Pherison turned his head back.

If Sexton Blake had been a less experienced hand at the game that night would have been his last on earth —and Tinker's, too, for Pherison had seen them and, at that moment, even though he had picked up the thread of his remark and was continuing to talk, he was at the same time giving a warning message to his two companions.

And without the shred of a warning, all Hades seemed to break loose.

Archie Pherison started it by throwing himself sideways and clawing a heavy revolver from beneath his robe. Reggie Fetherston and Algy Somerton were almost as fast on the draw; and then a fusillade of bullets came shattering against the half-open door behind which Blake and Tinker were standing. And following that first volley, the light in the room went out.

Darkness —dead, menacing abyssmal darkness. In one cell-like room three of the most ruthless criminals living —in the other, Sexton Blake and Tinker. And all five beings knowing that sudden vicious death was over them. Just what followed could only be told if one could get the version from each one of the five who was there.

To Blake and Tinker it seemed as if the night had gone mad. Blake was the first to take the offensive after that first volley, and as he dropped low to shoot into the other room, Tinker swung to the edge of the door and began firing over his head.

They worked the triggers of their automatics like things possessed, spraying the place with a leaden hail, and then they flung back again as three weapons flashed beyond in the darkness. The bullets thudded against the door, and, so far, they were both safe; but they did not know whether they had made a bit or not.

There was the sound of a voice beyond the door, and then, fearing that the quarry would escape by some door there (Blake did not know then that they must come through the room in which he and Tinker stood to get to the ground above) he risked using the torch.

Pulling it out he gave a word to Tinker, and then, while he held it in his left hand and switched it on, both he and the lad began shooting again.

The beam showed a strange sight. Crouching behind one bed was Archie Pherison with his gun pointing towards them, and the moment the torch flashed he began to shoot. At one side was Reggie Fetherston lying prone, and in that single glance Blake knew that they had got one at least.

He had not time to pick out Somerton before he had to switch off, and then there came a yell from one of the bandits, and he had just time to shout to Tinker, when the rush came. The door was driven back forcibly —there was a terrific commotion in the place, and flash after flash and roar after roar as the guns spoke.

Blake and Tinker were both shooting at close quarters now, but wildly, for it was impossible to tell exactly where the foe was so quickly did the location of the flashes change. But then in a slight pause, Blake heard the clatter of heels on iron, and once more he jerked out the torch.

As he flashed it on he caught sight of Archie Pherison racing up a winding iron staircase, while Algy Somerton was just disappearing through the door through which he and Tinker had come from the secret passage.

"After him," he yelled to Tinker. "Here's the torch. I will take the other."

Tinker grabbed the torch and made for the pivotal stone door, while Blake raced up the iron staircase after Pherison. Tinker held the light focussed until Blake disappeared, then he squeezed through into the passage, and stood for a moment until he could hear the rattle of Somerton's heels on the stone. He caught a glimpse of light for a second, and knew from that that the bandit also had a torch, and had just turned the bend in the passage.

Tinker had to pause long enough to slip a new clip into his automatic, for he knew it would be madness to go in pursuit with an empty weapon; then he started after the fugitive, watching at each bend in case of ambush.

But what he did not know was that Algy Somerton had also emptied his weapon, and had no more cartridges to recharge.

Tinker followed as fast as he dared, and from time to time caught the gleam of the other's torch which was enough to tell him that he was on the right track.

Once the fugitive passed the spot where the passage branched, and kept straight on, Tinker knew he was making for the river. He increased his speed a little when he found that Somerton did not pause to shoot back, and by then he was beginning to guess the truth. But Somerton was still running ahead of him when he reached the end of the bridge where the roof of the passage grew suddenly low, and when he came in sight of the hollow beneath the stone pier Tinker was just in time to see the fugitive crossing the plank.

Tinker stopped and sent a couple of shots at the bandit. His hand was shaking from excitement of the fight and the chase, and he missed, and that miss was just enough to give Algy Somerton time to catch hold of the plank and push it off the edge into the water beneath. Then he disappeared through the doorway leading to the passage which led to the cellar beneath the inn on the island.

Tinker gave a cry of rage as he saw what the other had done, but as he reached the edge of the ledge and measured the distance across he jerked half aloud:

"It can be done, and I can do it. He must not escape."

With that he backed up a dozen feet or so, and then with a run he took off from the sheer edge of the ledge and landed with less than three inches to spare on the other side. He balanced precariously for a few moments, but finally recovered himself, and pushing through the doorway, went racing along towards the cellar.

Somerton had been in such a hurry that he had not taken the time to close the other stone door, and, as he squeezed through, Tinker made for the stairs up which he knew the other must have gone.

He reached the room above —the one which gave out on to the garden —and there he paused abruptly as he saw the gendarme who had been left in charge of the inn lying unconscious on the floor. Somerton had jumped him without warning, and had knocked him cold with the butt end of his weapon.

Tinker hurdled the still form and dashed out into the garden. He ran towards the edge of the revetment and was just in time to see a figure pushing off in the skiff by which he and Blake had come. He lifted his automatic and began shooting, and at the sound of the shots the gendarmes on the bridge began to blow their whistles. But almost at the same moment a tug going down river began to hoot too, and the sound of the police whistles was drowned in the uproar.

Tinker ran along the revetment shooting as he ran, but while he knew he must have hit the boat several times the man in it still kept rowing with all his might. Despite his efforts, Tinker saw him sweep through the narrow channel between the island on which he stood and the other two below and then he saw nothing but a dark blotch as the boat got farther and farther out into the river.

He made his way back to the inn and found that several gendarmes from the bridge had come down. In a few words he explained what had happened, and some of them raced off to warn those on duty at the other end of the bridge to be on the lookout for the fugitive on that side.

But it may be said here, that while the skiff with half-a-dozen bullet holes through it was found full of water against the bank on the opposite side the following morning, there was no sign of the fugitive. Soon after getting clear, he had discovered that the skiff had been holed several times beneath the water line, and he knew he could not get far in it. But he too had heard that screaming of the tug whistle, and as he pulled across the river he saw a dark blotch appear in front of him. Then there came another and another, and he knew that the tug was towing several loaded barges downstream.

He rowed as close as he dared, then he slipped into the water, abandoning the boat, and swam for the last barge. He managed to reach it in time to grasp the helm and thus, clinging to the great rudder, he was carried on down the Seine, past Villennes, past Triel and on to Maulan, where he slipped quietly away and made the shore. By daybreak he had covered several miles towards the coast, and three days later he managed to make the yacht Sultan which lay in the harbour of Havre.

When Somerton disappeared Tinker, deeply chagrined over the escape, made his way back through the secret passage to the room where the fight had started. As he squeezed through the door he heard voices, and then as he crossed the first room he saw that the other cell-like apartment was crowded with men.

He entered, and the first thing his eyes took in was Blake stretched out on one of the cots with someone bending over him. He hurried forward and gave a cry of relief as he saw that Blake was conscious.

"They got me in the shoulder," said Blake, reading the question in his eyes. "What of Somerton?"

"I am sorry, sir, but he got away," answered Tinker. "He was ahead of me the whole way and the gendarme at the inn couldn't stop him. He got clear with our skiff by the river, but the gendarmes are trying to pick him up."

Blake nodded.

"They may catch him yet," he said. "Anyway, it isn't your fault, and we have the other two, so it isn't so bad."

Just then the group of gendarmes shifted, and Tinker could see the other two cots. On one lay Archie Pherison, his face as white as a sheet and his eyes closed. He glanced towards Blake, who said:

"It was just after he got me in the shoulder that I brought him down. The doctor here says it is in the body, but doesn't know how bad it is yet. It was in the lane above. He got that far and was making for the gate. Even at that he brought down two of the gendarmes."

"And Fetherston?" asked Tinker, looking at the other cot where the third bandit lay, also with closed eyes.

"A smashed shoulder, so they say," replied Blake. "And we have the whole caboodle of loot, my lad," he went on, speaking still in English. "That is why I don't mind this wound."

"Where was it, guv'nor?" asked Tinker quickly.

"In this room under the beds," replied Blake, and again as he looked Tinker saw three large leather bags against the wall.

There is little more to tell of the mystery of the house on the river. That night Blake was taken to the local hospital where his wound was given every attention, and in adjoining beds were Archie Pherison and Reggie Fetherston with two gendarmes to each cot, fully armed and taking no chances on their escaping though they were wounded.

M. Dupuis, the Prefect, motored down from Paris on hearing the news, and stayed over night to take Blake and Tinker back when he heard that the doctor would permit the detective to be moved. Blake was right in saying that they had recovered the loot, for, on checking up, it was found that nearly everything that had been taken during the whole series of outrages was in those bags ready, as Blake and Tinker knew, to be taken from Poissy that night.

For the time being, the two Musketeers who had been shot down would have to remain in hospital under arrest, but as soon as they could be moved the Prefect said they would be taken to Paris, and, in view of the fact that they had killed, he assured Blake that they would go to the guillotine.

As for Algy Somerton, nothing was heard of him, and when he realised that one of that desperate trio was still at large, Sexton Blake thought privately that he would not like to bet too much money on the execution coming off until he saw the two criminals actually under the sombre guillotine.

But that was for the future, and just then he had no further time to devote to the mystery of the house on the river, for despite the wound in his shoulder, there were urgent matters in London awaiting his attention.

Nevertheless, as he read Tinker's detailed record of the case in the famous Index, he was glad that opportunity had once more offered for him to cross weapons with the Three Musketeers, and if the two now under arrest went to the guillotine as the Prefect said they would, then he promised himself that later on he would lay Algy Somerton by the heels as well.

A sentiment with which Tinker fervently agreed.

THE END.
[51500 WORDS]

Please order next month's numbers of the Sexton Blake Library NOW! See page ii of cover.

OUR MAGAZINE CORNER.

When the specialist branch of the police —the detective force — came into existence, the value of specialisation began to dawn on the crooks in a most painful manner. Up to then, the crook who "did" some particular form of crime well and stuck to it, refusing to engage in any other branch of criminality, was an astonishing exception.

To-day the specialist crook is the rule. The lowest of the underworld —sneak-thieves who rob children going on an errand with a copper or two stuffed in their hot little hands —even has its trade union. The practitioners of that most despicable art specialise in their job, knowing that in that direction lies their greatest chance of salvation from the police and the sleuths of "the Yard."

It is the crook who is "Jack of all trades" and master of none whom the arms of the law grips soonest. But even for the cleverest of the specialist criminals there is little hope for long. For detectives specialise, too, and narrow their studies of crime down to the one phase which it is their ambition to combat.

The letter-box thief, for instance, has his own particular enemy at the Yard —several, in fact. They endeavour always to think ahead of the letter-box robbers, and have ready a ruse to defeat any new move invented by the pests of the pillar-box.

These crooks rob his Majesty's pillar-boxes as easily almost as you might open a baby's money-box. A length of springy whalebone, bent at the lower end so as to scoop up the letters when the apparatus is pushed into the pillar-box, brings the posted letters and small packets within reach of the crooks fingers. He pockets them and inspects the contents at leisure.

For confederate he has another crook specialist —a forger. The cheques and money orders taken from the purloined letters are manipulated by this scoundrel so as to bring them in a far larger sum; a stroke of the pen here, a dash there —and there a little dab of chemical to remove unwanted figures or writing, and the confederates in specialised crime glean a very fat harvest.

The crook who specialises in street pillar-boxes seldom strays into the province of the crook whose efforts are aimed at the letterboxes of big business firms and private houses. It is the private

123

house which attracts some of the last named specialists, who leave the more risky field, represented by the letter-boxes of business firms, to those who prefer to work it.

The commonest method adopted to extract letters from the inside door-mat is connected with the morning newspaper. The crook watches the paper-boy push the sheet not through the box but half-way under the street door.

Then he waits for the postman to come along and shoot a few letters through the slot. These fall on to the newspaper. The crook watches the postman out of sight —and the rest is easy. He simply pulls the newspaper carefully from beneath the bottom of the door and picks up the letters it brings with it.

Another instance of specialist crooks working hand-in-hand is presented by the jewel thief and the "fence," or receiver of stolen property. The thief has specialised amazingly in his methods.

Jewel thieves' tricks are innumerable, but the latest is not yet common enough to have passed into the repertoire of the ordinary crime specialist. It has to do with a sealed room, a chloroform pump, and some poor individual wearing or carrying a valuable load of precious stones.

It has just been practised in Paris. A luxuriously appointed drawing-room was so constructed as to enable the "villain of the piece," when he had lured his intended victim thereto, to seal all air inlets and outlets, and from an adjoining room pump chloroform, into the drawing-room till the unsuspecting guest lost consciousness.

In no branch of criminal practice perhaps has specialisation been more closely followed than in the "con man's" line. He has to be a swindler and a consummate actor —the finished article in both cases. When he can combine the two arts, he can consider himself a swindler specialist.

How is it, then, that with all this clever specialisation, so many crooks get caught —geniuses in their own line of craft? For the same reason that the brothers Bidwell and their confederate Macdonnell, after having roped in £100,000 by a complicated fraud —so complicated they thought no one on earth would ever be able to spot the precise working of it —came to grief over an omission on a forged bill.

They forgot to date it! They had concentrated on that fraud until they had become specialists, to all intents infallible. But the human

124

machine is no more reliable than one from an engineering shop. The three schemers recognised that painful fact when the missing date led to them being put away for a lengthy stretch of imprisonment.

R/R